A DARK TURN OF MIND

A NOVEL

ELLEN WEST

D1571095

And leave me if I'm feeling too lonely
Full as the fruit on the vine
You know some girls are bright as the morning
And some have a dark turn of mind

-"Dark Turn of Mind" by Gillian Welch

PROLOGUE

Present Day

I tend to get lost in other people. All it takes is for me to look at them and suddenly I *know* that person's entire life situation. Truly. Their stories sweep over me in waves, crashing against my psyche, spilling into my soul. As a general rule, I don't talk about this aspect of myself much, because it's really rather awkward to explain. It's as if I connect with other people on a whole other level, though to me that just sounds too "New Age". Reading people is simply something that I've always done, an ability I've always had. Just being near someone can trigger it, the energy radiating off of them transforms into images that fly through my brain in a matter of seconds. The man who just lost his job, thinking about suicide while he waits in line in front of me at the grocery store. The woman behind me in the bank who just found out she is pregnant. The teenager, busing my table, who can't stop thinking about what he shouldn't have done last night at the party. Simple things, often. Sometimes, not so simple.

Often, the energy I capture is light and engaging, happy news or falling in love. Other times it's dark and draining. Just this morning, for example, a woman drove by me while I was getting the morning paper from the street. She was driving a cranberry-colored pickup truck with one of those silver tool-boxes attached to the bed behind the cab. The truck was in fairly good shape, not terribly new, maybe half-a-decade old. The woman's dishwater blonde hair was hastily pulled back into a loose ponytail, her bangs falling over her face. A boy, around twelve years of age, was sitting beside her, leaning slightly forward, his buzzed blonde hair glinting in the bright morning sunlight. His eyes were wide, his hand on the dash, steadying himself because he hadn't removed his backpack in his haste to jump into the truck.

A gentle buzzing began to spread throughout my body and I knew right then that the truck had been taken that morning, in secret, after a long and harrowing night. Stolen in the early hours of the day while her husband 'slept it off'. A night of drinking and yelling and fighting and cruelty. Her son cowering in his room, pretending to be asleep, thinking of inflicting unspeakable acts upon his father. Burying the hurt in more hurt and deeper anger.

In my mind, I watched as the boy's mother silently crept into his room before the morning light. Quietly, she roused him from bed to dress and down a cup of cold juice and dry toast that caught in his throat with his tears. They moved like ghosts through the house, avoiding the darkness of the room at the end of the hall, lest they wake the slumbering beast. Her husband's jacket still lay in a pile on the kitchen floor from the night before. Reaching into the jacket to grab the keys, she almost gags from the stench of stale cigarette smoke and bad whiskey, the same smells she vigorously scrubbed from her body early this morning, while the water hid her angry tears. Outside, she started the truck while frantically wiping droplets of dew from the windshield and mirrors using the sleeves of her sweatshirt as a makeshift rag. With hands shaking and a purple bruise peeking out from the top of her shirt, she backed quietly out of the driveway. A weary smile to her son, meant to be comforting, just fuels the fire of hate in his belly. Unable to do anything about it at home, he will spend the day acting out in class.

All of those thoughts and pictures happen in a

matter of minutes. In the time that the mother and son have passed me by, I have absorbed all of that information. I watched the truck as it rolled to a stop at the end of my street and turned right. The truck, the people, the feeling---they were all gone.

I used to do a lot of reading about supernatural phenomena and psychological abnormalities. I read a lot about ghosts, past lives, psychics and empaths. About premonitions and deja vu and palmistry. About Tarot cards and Ouija boards. Horoscopes. My thoughts were thus: Of course. Of course, people could see the future, could sense things. Of course, you predict your day based on the stars. Why not? I did it every day. I believe my abilities came from my grandmother. When I was growing up, during lazy summers at her house, she had always been ready with a story about how she saw signs in the sky and had dreams about dead relatives. Talking about my dreams to her, the feelings that I got around people, she made it all seem normal. Commonplace. Others looked at it differently though. When I told them about the little gray boy that lived on our stairs, they ignored me. When I told them about the dark shadow that told me to do bad things, I was told not to lie. When I tried to kill myself, for the first time, at the age of twelve, they called it a phase.

If it had all only been that simple.

1

Mary's hand is caked with the blood she has been vomiting for days. She reaches out toward John as she struggles to catch her breath, buried beneath quilts and blankets in what was once their marriage bed, but had now become what she was sure would be her deathbed. Her eyes are red from crying and her lips are stained with the blood she has coughed up into the handkerchiefs and towels. She looks at him earnestly, pleading for help, for relief from the wretched vomiting that has consumed her. Jon holds her hand gently and tries to meet her gaze, but for all his heart, he could only see his late wife, Lucy. How could this happen again? How could he again lose the woman he loved? Mary cries softly, calling his name over and over again, in a weak, feeble voice. Jon pulls

Mary to him and holds her tightly. He rocks her body slowly back and forth, whispering, always whispering "I love you, I love you, I love you...Lucy."

2

My name is Sally Jane Riley. *SJ* for short. In my forty-one years on this earth, I've found that truth is often stranger than fiction, though fiction can often appear to be true. I'm an introvert, a dreamer, a storyteller prone to misgivings of the truth. To me, writers are amongst the bravest of people. While I don't consider myself a "true writer", I have written a multitude of poems and songs and stories, filling journal upon journal, that until this moment, I had kept all to myself, because to send the words out into the world would be to admit that they came from me. The sickness, the darkness, the unpalatable scenarios of darkness and death. I think that is what keeps me from becoming a true writer. The shame. The guilt. How people like Stephen King and Gillian Flynn and Lisa Gardner have gotten past it, I don't know.

Maybe because, for them, it really is pure imagination. There is no illness, no compulsion to relive the terrible visions and sensations from the abuse of my childhood to the continued abuse of my mind.

The urge to write is strong within me. I write like an addict uses, in small doses and large mind-numbing binges. On scrap papers and in tiny notebooks. On secret files in my computer and spoken through voice recordings on my phone. The writing comes in feverish bursts that consume me and wreck my soul. As the words pour out, I try to deny them, falling into the darkness that belies a sickness in my belly. I can feel the bile rising in my throat and a queasy feeling that drops down to my toes, carrying with it the fruits of my overactive imagination.

Although I loved writing, the jobs were few and far between. I became a librarian because I love the written word. Every day I am surrounded by writing--writing that unnerves, disturbs, inspires. The hours are good and in general, it's a pretty quiet and solitary job. I am an introvert at heart. Socializing physically hurts. My head, my stomach, my whole body vibrates. Making "small talk" is pure hell. In my head, I am constantly thinking: What should I say next? Do I look interested enough? Should I say something now? And more often, What did they say?. It's not that I don't try to listen. It's more an issue of there being such a ruckus going on in my head, that it's all that I can do to concentrate on the person's lips moving. If there is the slightest noise going on around me, I literally cannot hear what they are saying. I make a lot of inferences. Mostly, I'm right. Sometimes I'm wrong.

I enjoy stacking the returned books on the trolley and bringing them back to their rightful spots on the shelves. It's like solving a little mystery every day. Numbers have never really made sense to me, but those little combinations of numbers and letters on the binding of the book jackets always make me feel safe. J338.52? Yup, it goes right here between J338.51 and J338.53. Every time. No exceptions. I like to read the titles as I go, mostly because I'm always on the look-out for a good book. I tend to only read mysteries, and then only mysteries by female writers. Not that I am sexist, I just feel safer with a woman writer somehow. James Patterson and Tess Gerritsen can write the same violent, sexually suggestive, scene, but somehow I feel that at least if Tess wrote it, she knows how a woman would really feel in that situation. How I've felt in those situations.

Today was just like any other day. Mundane, really. I finished my shift at the library and left to go sit in the ever-increasing traffic problem that is consuming our little town of Waxhaw, North Carolina. It started to drizzle, and the traffic was already piling up, so I ended up turning right out of the street and then left into the parking lot of Emmett's restaurant in order to merge into the lane of traffic heading out of town. The light drizzle had turned to rain, which made me smile because I like listening to the rain softly tap on the windows. It puts me in a relaxed, almost meditative state. Traffic was already at a standstill, so I leaned back in the chair a bit, slipped the gear into Park, and closed my eyes, just to rest them. The gentle pitter-pat of the raindrops, coupled intermittent sweep of the windshield wipers, lulled me to sleep in a manner of seconds.

In my mind I pictured myself walking through a house. An older house, with a steep stairway. As I am about to step up onto the stairs, a man with short dark hair comes rushing down, clutching a bundled and stained white sheet under his arm. He is wearing a long-sleeved coat, dark in color, with a high neckline. His hair looks like it has been recently cut, the ends sticking out and reaching for the sky as if they had been suddenly relieved of a heavy burden. He is sweating, beads of it dripping down his forehead and dropping off the bridge of his nose. He smells hot, dirty, almost musky. As he rushes by me, sleeves rolled up, I notice a smudge of red on his forearm by his wrist. It looks wet and sticky and matches the stains on the sheet.

He seems to take no notice of me and hurries off. Curious, about where he had come from, I continued up the stairs. The steps groan and complain under the stress of my weight. The top landing is cluttered with more discarded linens and what looked like underclothes. All of the doors are closed. I walk to the first door, on my right, and try the handle. Locked. I move to the next door, on my left. Same. I am about to reach for the third when there is a loud scream. I freeze in my spot. The scream is followed by a low moan and the sound of someone vomiting. Frightened, I turn back toward the stairs and begin to rush down. Just as I reach the landing, I hear a loud honking noise.

I am jolted awake. At first, I was disoriented. The windshield had become a warbly mess, glazed over with what was now a deluge of rain. Quickly, I realized that the traffic was now moving and that I had indeed fallen asleep for a brief moment. The car in front of me was at least two car lengths ahead. The man behind me, in the plumbing company van, flipped me off as he swerved around me on the left and continued ahead. I nodded, gave him a sarcastic 'thumbs up', put my car in gear, and fell back into line.

3

At home, I groggily walked through the front door and headed toward the kitchen. Placing my bag on the back of a barstool, I walked over to the refrigerator and poured myself a glass of sweet tea. Tea in hand, I headed to the back porch to relax. The porch is one of my favorite places in the house. The walls are painted a deep sage-green color that seems to breathe on rainy days like today. The color emphasized the grayness and the sadness of the rain. Somehow, I found that comforting---the sadness of the room. I was still vaguely sleepy, in the way that you are when you take a nap but are awakened too early. I let my thoughts drift to my dream. I could still smell the stench of the man's sweat. I remembered the look of angst on his face and thought that maybe he was a butler who was afraid of being scolded. Or maybe, given the vomiting I heard, I had seen a glimpse of life during an epidemic; the frantic washing and scrubbing and changing of sheets.

Except that it felt more ominous than that.

I placed my tea on the side table by the chair I was sitting in, rose from my seat, and went inside for a moment to grab my notebook. It is never far from where I am. I carry it in my messenger bag to take out whenever I have a few moments to write. I use it to jot down the little story ideas and poems that came to me during the day. I opened my bag and rummaged around inside until I felt its smooth cover. I pulled the black leather-bound notebook out of my bag and unclipped the pen from its perch in the loop on its side. I wrote down the dream as best as I could remember it. Something about it seemed oddly important. I thought to myself that maybe it could be the start of a short story.

I was about to lose myself in more writing when I heard the front door open. My husband, Evan, was home from work.

"Hey Beautiful, what are you up to?" he questioned and smiled as he leaned down for a peck on the cheek. I caught a glimpse of our reflection in the mirror that hung opposite the kitchen table. His hair was still blonde, not even a touch of grey. His muscular build and the goatee with a touch of strawberry blonde---he was still as handsome as ever.

"Just jotting a few things down," I said as I closed my notebook. He looked at me as if he was going to say something, then didn't. Things have been like that between us recently. It's as if something is on the tip of his tongue, but he just can't spit it out. We are usually so honest with each other, but lately, there is a distance between us. I smiled at him and kissed his cheek.

"Ready for dinner?" I asked, heading to the kitchen counter to stir the soup in the crockpot. Thursdays were my late nights which meant convenience cooking for the both of us. "I just have to heat the bread in the oven for a few minutes and everything will be ready."

He mentioned needing to change and went upstairs. I popped a loaf of pre-baked bread into the oven to finish and gathered the bowls and spoons for our meal. The dream came to mind again and I couldn't shake the feeling that I'd been in that house before.

4

Friday morning came quickly, much too quickly for my taste. I pulled the sheets up over my head and buried my face in my pillow as Evan got up to face the day. He turned on the radio in the bathroom, blasted the Howard Stern Show, and got in the shower. I did not feel like moving, let alone getting up and going to work. I just want to disappear, to cease to exist, to just fade away into a comforting mist and feel my body dissipate like tiny rain particles. But duty called.

Once downstairs, I threw some dishes in the dishwasher and actually remembered to start it that time. I grabbed my keys and messenger bag off the kitchen table and headed out the door. A familiar numbness started to overtake me. A blank feeling, as if my whole body was turning gray. The voice, her voice, started to drum through my head. *Worthless. Lazy. Stupid. Kill yourself. Just end it already.* I try to deny her existence, but she is very persistent. It's part of my diagnosis, but to me, she's just a part of who I am. I don't always hear her, and sometimes she's jumbled by other voices, other noises, but she's always there. I can feel her even when she's sleeping.

Ten years ago, I was diagnosed with a form of schizophrenia called schizoaffective disorder. It sounds more ominous than it really is, I think. But then, maybe I'm just used to how things are. At first, I was very resistant to my diagnosis, the doctors, the hospitals, and medications. Gradually, I learned to trust the doctors and began to take my medications and the symptoms grew manageable. I grew more manageable. I had been a terrible mess before, ever since the miscarriage of my only pregnancy. I had a breakdown in the hospital while recovering and was not allowed to go home until I had an appointment with an established psychiatrist. Despite taking my medication, I still have mood swings and visual and auditory hallucinations. Mostly because I refuse to go on the higher doses of the medications the psychiatrist recommends. In the hospital, the dose of medication they gave me was so high, it made me feel like a zombie. I felt cut off from myself and everyone else around me. From the hospital, I was released into my first psychiatrist, Dr. Aisley's care. It was tough at first, being told what to do and having to depend on medication to function, but Dr. Aisley and I found common ground; I would take my medications religiously and he wouldn't prescribe anything too sedating.

When we moved to North Carolina, the first thing I had to do was navigate our new insurance and blindly find a reputable psychiatrist. And a therapist. Back in Massachusetts, Dr. Aisley had been both for me, as a favor. Now I had to deal with two strangers, instead of one. After some trial and error, I finally found Dr. Hill and Elizabeth Benson. They both turned out to be really helpful.

The drive to the library was uneventful, and when I arrived, things were quiet. I shuffled the trolley about, putting the books away. I cleared up the toys in the children's corner. I cleaned up the DVD aisle and alphabetized the DVDs that were out of place. Around mid-morning, I volunteered to go out and collect the books from the return bin outside. The reluctant sun had popped out from behind the clouds and I felt that the natural light and fresh air might jolt me back into myself.

The ground was damp and the sun shone on the droplets in the grass, making them sparkle like tiny jewels. I could smell the ripeness of the Earth, the pungent-sweet odor of the newly trimmed grass, and the deep, dark tones of the dirt in the flower beds. The sidewalk was a work of art as patterns emerged between the wet and drying areas of cement. I turned the key in the back of the old metal return bin to unlock the box and several books toppled out onto the sidewalk. I cursed under my breath at the damp spot on the pavement just below the open door and hoped that the pages wouldn't wick up the moisture and ruin the books. The library is notorious in its propensity for "personal accountability," as in "paying for your mistakes"---quite literally. Christ, I hated having to pay for library books. The library always charges you three times as much as the book is worth if you consider most of our popular titles could be found at thrift shops and yard sales.

As I scooped up the books, I noticed a woman out of the corner of my eye, and that familiar buzzing took over my body. She was across the parking lot, with her back to me, her dark hair cascading in loose curls down her back. She was wearing a long pale white dressing gown that looked extremely out of date. She was facing the elementary school that stands about fifty feet before her, across the street from the library. I thought maybe she was a parent, here to bring her child a forgotten lunch, when I noticed that she was barefoot. As I adjusted my weight to pull myself up off my knees for a better look, I knocked the metal door of the dropbox wide open and it clanked loudly into the metal book trolley. I leaned forward to grab the trolley cart before it rolled off, looked back, and the woman was gone. A cool breeze blew past me and ruffled my bangs loose from behind my ears. I hastily brushed them back and turned back to the bin as a solitary crow landed in the center of the parking lot.

I was just about to toss another book on the trolley when I noticed the title. *The Crucible* by Arthur Miller. It had been a long time since I'd read it, but I remembered the movie. Winona Ryder and Daniel Day-Lewis. New England in the Fall, when the Witches come alive again. Autumn is my favorite time of year, something about the crackling leaves and the beauty in the dying all around us. I use the edge of my t-shirt to wipe the water droplets from the wet pavement off of the cover of the book, place it on the trolley, and chilled, I hurry back inside.

5

Sunday has always been my favorite day of the week. Most people like Fridays or Saturdays, but I'm more of a Sunday girl. I actually liked that horrid pit-of-your-stomach feeling that you get, when you know that Monday is calling from just around the corner. I liked rainy Sundays the best, and Mother Nature was only too happy to oblige today. I was home bustling about the house, trying to keep my mind off my troubles. Evan had fallen asleep on the couch watching a soccer game. The house was peaceful. I quietly poured myself some cold coffee leftover from the morning and popped it into the microwave. Gathering my grey knit cardigan around me, I opened the sliding glass doors and stepped out onto the back porch.

The backyard was alive with color. The rain made

the trees pop. I could hear the soft droplets hitting the roof above and watched their teardrop trails down the window panes. I crossed the porch and opened the two front windows halfway so that I could hear the birds as they called each other. I sat in the lounge chair and pulled my cardigan closed around me as I sipped and savored the coffee. While it was cool out, it wasn't too chilly, so I settled back into the chair and stared out the window at the squirrels raiding my bird feeder.

My symptoms have been worsening lately. That can happen with my diagnosis, highs and lows, good days and bad. This morning, I could feel myself disconnecting from my surroundings. It's an odd sensation, but not unpleasant. I can only liken it to back in the days when we only had landlines and you could hear another conversation breaking through, while you were on the phone. I used to love that. I'd be talking with my best friend Katie, and suddenly you could hear a faint conversation in the background. Usually a neighbor, but sometimes we couldn't tell who it was. The best times were when it got loud enough so that you could actually hear what the other people were saying, rather than just incoherent mumbling. We would be in the middle of the latest gossip, but as soon as we heard a breakthrough we would stop talking and just listen. For hours.

Tying up the phone line. That was before call waiting. My parents would get really irritated.

The disconnecting I feel is kind of like that. I experience a persistent faint mumbling in the back of my mind, then, out of the blue, sometimes I'll get a day when my mind is so quiet I feel I have no thoughts. It doesn't usually bother me, I've gotten used to it. One of the benefits I get at work is to use my earbuds to listen to music when I'm getting anxious. Only my boss knows why I do it, and I try to keep the times that I use the privilege to few and far between. If I'm listening to music like that, it's because the voices have gotten too loud. The music helps to distract me. Mostly, though, I do like listening to what the voices say. Outside of one particular voice, they mostly seem harmless. Sometimes, too, the conversations are wonderfully odd. Once I heard an entire debate about the benefits of putting household forks on one's windowsill to keep aliens out. I did it that very night.

Lately, though, *She* has been getting belligerent. The one dark voice, the girl that grew up inside me. As a child, she told me her name was Irene. Lately, she's been sitting and watching me. Whispering terrible things. She sits in the middle of the floor, curled up on herself, with her legs tucked under her but her eyes are always on me. Her hair is short, bright blonde, pixie cut, but not well. She always wears the same pale blue dress. Her eyes are bewitching. Grey. Cold. Like a cloud-laden sky.

I could feel her coming. I lay quietly in the lounge chair and tried to ignore her. Then, there she was again. Out of the corner of my eye, I could see her sitting to the left of the potted peace plant in the corner. She was almost hidden by one of its larger leaves. I could see the top of her head and the tips of her toes. And her eyes. They were stern.

I turned and stared straight forward. I started naming the things I saw in front of me, in my head. Robin. Birch tree. Red Maple. Another Robin. Chickadee. It's a coping mechanism I learned in the hospital. Naming things in your environment can help bring you back to the moment, and help distract from the hallucinations. I got the uneasy feeling that someone was right next to me. Too close. I braced myself. Suddenly, the hairs on my arms stood up and I felt dizzy. I sat up straight and spilled my coffee down the front of my shirt onto my yoga pants. I wiped my stomach and legs where the coffee was starting to stain with a blanket that had been on the chair. Without a backward glance, I got up, left the porch, and shut the door.

6

I awoke suddenly at 5:30 in the morning and stared at the ceiling, watching the faint morning light try to cast away shadows from the night before. My sleep had been restless, my dreams vivid, but forgettable. I had always thought that I was in charge of my illness, in a way. Even as a young child, I had coping strategies. Wearing a rubber band on my wrist to snap me back to reality. Journaling. Praying. In college, it had been recommended by a professor that I "seek counseling." I didn't. I had always felt in control, no matter how out of control my thoughts were. But now, now I wasn't so sure of myself.

I desperately wanted to reach across the bed and wake my husband. Tell him that the voices were getting worse. Tell him that I was seeing people that aren't there. Tell him that I thought of suicide too many times during the day to count. But I kept silent. That's the problem with mental illness. No matter how much you want to talk about what's happening to you, no matter how much you want help, nobody really understands, nobody can really help. The only person that can help you, is you. That is the sad and scary truth.

I forced myself to sit up and pull on my robe. I shuffled down the hall and blindly made my way downstairs to start the coffee. I flipped on the TV for distraction, the images flashing like firecrackers in the darkened kitchen. I stood up on my tiptoes to reach the coffee filters, teetering against the counter because I am too short. The filters tumbled away from my clumsy fingers, further into the cabinet. As I leaned in closer, steadying my arm and lifting my back foot off the floor, a harsh whisper sounded in my left ear.

"Help me!"

My hand slipped and my head smacked hard against the bottom of the cabinet door. I let out an audible, "Fuck!," and reached up to rub the throbbing pain. I looked around the kitchen, thinking, hoping that maybe it was the tv. An infomercial for a countertop toaster oven droned on. I shivered, crossing my arms and hugging myself. The room was freezing cold.

I looked around the kitchen once more, just to be sure nobody was there. I shook off the tingly feeling that was slowly taking over my body and grabbed a stool from the pantry in order to reach the fallen coffee filters. I started the coffee machine and sat down to watch the news for a bit before my husband would be up.

7

We have only lived in our new home for about three months. It's a beautiful, five-bedroom bungalow, on one of the larger lots in the development. I hadn't wanted to live in a "neighborhood;" I preferred the privacy of a lot of trees and miles of land between me and the nearest neighbor. But, the price was right, so here we were. I had to admit, the house is perfect for us and I found myself loving it, despite the proximity of my neighbors.

We had moved in the middle of Summer, in North Carolina, so it had been hot. I hadn't yet really taken any time to explore the neighborhood. This beautiful October day was my first day off in a while. The morning was crisp, and the sky shone Carolina blue. Once Evan left I grabbed my cream-colored cardigan and headed out the door. I walked eastward, down towards the newer part of the development. The developers kept most of the trees, so the scenery was alive with color. I felt my spirits lifting as I walked through a rainfall of red and golden leaves brought down by a gust of wind. I rounded the corner by a particularly impressive stucco house and discovered a trail half-hidden by the trees. My curiosity got the better of me. I ventured off the cement pathway and started to follow the shallow indentation between the trees.

Though the whole area was overgrown with weeds and small bushes, there was definitely a path, and if you looked closely, you could just make it out. I looked up and saw that it went all the way up the hill-side and behind the neighborhood. Taking a deep breath of cool, autumn air, I decided to follow it.

I was breathing pretty hard as I neared the top. My palms were scraped, and the knees of my jeans muddied, where I had tripped over old roots and brambles. The path just ended at the top of the hill. The trees were thinner there, opening up into a large clearing. The grass was waist high and I stepped into it like wading into an ocean. I rested my palms at the top of the grasses, letting their tips tickle my hands as I walk. The sensation was intoxicating and I closed my eyes and breathed the air and felt happy in my soul for the first time in weeks. All of the darkness seemed to fade away as I turned my face up to the sky, letting the sun kiss my cheeks.

Suddenly, my foot struck something hard and I came down to Earth with a crash. Heralding my second "Fuck!" of the day, I pushed myself back up, spitting dirt from my mouth and tried to get my bearings. No trees, so it couldn't have been another damn root. I turned to sit on my bottom, dusting off the knees of my pants, and faced the direction from which I had come. The sun sparkled on something gray, about a foot or so in front of where I was sitting. A rock, I had tripped on a rock in the middle of all of this greenery! I stood up and looked back on my path. Now, I had a much better view of my granite nemesis. My breath caught in my throat. I could barely make out a letter carved in the top of the stone. Two letters, actually.

I took the few steps that brought me closer to the stone. Upon closer inspection, I could see the initials M.A. A footstone? I looked around again, parting the grasses like the Red Sea, searching for the corresponding headstone. Nothing. I took a few steps to the right and found a larger stone. Not quite two feet tall and leaning at an angle that put it far below the tips of the grasses. A headstone. Oh, my God! This one said it belonged to Emily Todd, 1835-1912.

I felt like Alice in Wonderland in the scene where she's looking through the garden and keeps coming upon unwelcoming flowers. The stones glared out at me from under the sea of green. Now that I saw them, I didn't know how I could have missed them. I counted at least eleven, all in varying degrees of decay. You could see the carvings of the names and dates on most, but some were so worn that they were almost impossible to read. It was strange though, I could find the pairs of head and footstones to all of the grave markers, except the one that bore the initials M.A. I could only find the footstone. Teenagers, I figured, must've run off with the headstone.

I sat back down in the tall grass, next to the lone footstone, and looked up at the sky. The wind had picked back up and a flock of black crows was circling and swooping overhead. I started to feel dizzy. I closed my eyes for a minute and waited for the voices to come. Nothing. I opened my eyes and saw a shadow dart through the grasses shortly ahead of me. I started, thinking that maybe it was a fox or a large dog.

I stood up, started walking back towards the

forest, towards home. I felt like somebody was watching me and my skin started to prickle. I told myself not to turn around. I could feel her screams though. They shot through my soul like a bullet with butterfly wings.

8

At work the next day, I decided to spend my lunch break playing detective. While visions of sifting through dusty historical documents a-la-Indiana-Jones danced in my head, I figured that the easiest place to start was at my computer. I googled "Waxhaw" and "Cemeteries." I hit the jackpot. It listed the Waxhaw Cemetery, Waxhaw South Side Cemetery, Waxhaw City Cemetery, and Waxhaw Baptist Church Cemetery to name a few. Now, I just had to figure out which one lay dormant in my neighborhood.

Unfortunately, none of Google's cemeteries was my cemetery. I should've known it wasn't going to be that easy. It looked as if I'd have my dance with the historical documents after all. I had about ten minutes left on my lunch break, so I did a quick library search for relevant books and printed the list out to look through later.

During lunch, I hungrily ate the rest of my turkey sandwich and took a few good gulps of sweet tea. Wiping my mouth on the back of my cardigan sleeve like a child, I tossed my trash in the bin and headed to the front desk for my book trolley.

I was halfway into the front lobby when I smelled her perfume. Jean Nate. I knew because my grandmother used to wear the same scent. It came in a happy, yellow bottle with black dots. The cap itself was a huge black dot, which I found fascinating as a child. The scent was something akin to baby powder and overly pungent floral perfume. The smell of Jean Nate meant that Gladys Fletcher was in for her weekly reading materials.

Gladys Fletcher was a sweet elderly woman in her late 80s who had lived here in Waxhaw for her entire life. Her family roots sank deep into the area, back to the 1690s when Waxhaw was known only as the "Wisacky Area." Both she and her parents had worked in the Rodman-Heath Cotton Mill before it's closing in 1946. After that, she became a full-time housewife to her husband. As she had told me, they were never blessed with children, but she had several nieces and nephews. She wasn't your typical genteel Southern Lady; Gladys states that she's known too much of "hard times" to be a lady. She'd spent the last 20 years of her life taking care of her ailing and disabled husband until he passed in 2010.

Gladys and I connected one day, about a month ago, over a mystery novel. I was stocking the shelves and she had been dutifully tracing her finger over the bindings in the mystery section, looking for a good read. I don't usually just strike up random conversations, but something about her made me want to talk to her. I felt a gentle sadness behind her smile and had flashes of her leaning over an elderly man in a sleigh bed with a flowered quilt pulled up to his neck. There were medication bottles on the nightstand and a bag of liquid on a hook injected into his arm by a long thin tube and needle. I asked if she needed help finding something. She said, "Yes, a good book to take my mind off of things." I was only too happy to help. Since then, whenever Gladys came in to restock her book pile, we would always chat for a few minutes about the new books by our favorite authors.

"Sally Jane, dear," she crooned "got any good books for me?"

I smiled and let her hug me. She's one of the few people, outside of my family, that I'll allow that close. I got almost a heady high off of her perfume. It transported me right back into my grandmother's arms. Back home.

"There's a new Lisa Gardiner I don't think you've read," I said and smiled. I took her arm and helped guide her by the elbow as we walked slowly back to the mystery section. She chatted idly about her nieces and nephews and her garden, as I selected the book and took her arm again to guide her back to the front desk. She asked me to grab a few other titles from the back room that she had on hold. When I returned she was looking at me strangely.

"Are you okay, Dear?" she asked. Her eyes were warm and inviting, like the blue-green oceans of Southern Mexico.

"Yeah, fine," I said. I wasn't sure what she was getting at.

"Oh, it's just that you were back there for an awfully long time. I thought maybe the books hadn't come in after all."

I stared at her for a second, waiting for the punchline. Sometimes the old bird told some weird jokes. But nothing. I looked up at the clock. Over ten minutes had passed since I left Gladys at the counter. I remembered because when I had glanced at the clock it was a quarter to one and I was thinking that I only had a little less than two hours to go till quitting time.

"I'm sorry," I was tripping over my words, "I...I got a phone call while I was back there. I should've had somebody else bring you the books." I hadn't, but it sounded plausible.

"No worries, dear," she said, patting my hand. Her skin felt paper-thin and softer than powder. "I was just wondering."

And with that, she gathered up her books, placed them in her cloth shopping bag, and left the building.

I sat down in the chair behind the check-in computer and stared blankly at the screen. It had been a while since I had lost time like that. It's a scary feeling, not knowing what you have been doing. I figured I couldn't have gotten into too much mischief in the back room, but I was mortified at the thought that a coworker could've walked in on me standing there, staring blankly at nothing. I took a deep breath and sighed, then reached over to check in the books from the return bin.

9

There were some errands I needed to run after I got home that evening, even though I loathed the crowded grocery stores. The shelves weren't going to restock themselves, and we were in need of staples like paper towels and toilet paper. My husband was coming in the door as I was coming out. I felt like I hadn't seen him in days.

"Everything okay?" he asked.

I tried to smile despite the moment. "Yeah, things are great," I quipped sarcastically. He put his hand on my arm and turned me to look in his eyes.

"Are you sure you're okay?" his eyes were wide with concern. I wanted so badly to fall into his arms and cry.

"I'm fine, honey. I promise," I lied.

"Alright," he gave me a resigned look, "I'll throw some burgers on the grill for when you get back?"

"Of course, I'd like that," I answered. We held each other's gaze for a moment longer. So much went unsaid.

I mouthed a hurried, "Love You," to my husband and got into the car. I started the car and put on NPR. The evening news was in progress. I ran to the grocery store, my mind a flurry of snippets from the day's events. I needed to head back to the library. I hadn't had a chance to grab those books I had looked up and I was restless for answers.

The library stays open late on Wednesdays and Thursdays to accommodate the increase in the use of free computers and the internet. I love the library at night. The dim lights. The smell of the books. The quiet. Even the furniture is comforting, with its leather-bound chairs and long, solid oak tables. I chose a computer off in the corner by the historical reference section and took out my list. There were about five books on it. I started my search.

It turned out that most of the books on my list were really just pamphlets. Pages slightly yellowed. Even a little bit dusty. I guessed that not many people were brushing up on their History of Waxhaw this month.

The first pamphlet was titled, *The Tirzah Pres-*

byterian Church Cemetery, Waxhaw, NC, and had been compiled by the staff of the Dickerson Genealogy and Local History Room of the Union County Public Library.

The next pamphlet was titled, *The Waxhaws Chapter National Society Daughters of the American Colonists, Monroe, NC.* It was compiled by the Daughters of American Colonists Chapter, Waxhaw 1969. Monroe borders Waxhaw, so there might be some overlapping information in there.

The third pamphlet was titled, *History of Union County*, by Hayne Nelson Walden.

The next item was an actual book. *A Pictorial History of Union County,* North Carolina, was compiled by its contributors Brenda Helms and *The Enquirer-Journal.*

The last was an old town directory with several map pages throughout. I flipped through the book, carefully turning the tea-colored pages. Mostly information about watersheds and farm boundaries. Then I found it. The area that had become our neighborhood. There was a church marked on the page, "Blessed Name Baptist Church." That had to be the source of the cemetery, as they were often coupled to churches. And it would explain why the clearing was so big. I scrawled the name on a sheet of scrap paper with one of those tiny, yellow, No. 2 pencils that only libraries and mini-golf establishments are fond of, folded it, and placed it in my pocket.

That night, while I was sleeping, I heard the dog enter the room and pad across the rug to my side of the bed. I was in that foggy state, between waking and dreaming, where you can sense your surroundings, but not necessarily make sense of them. After a few minutes, I realized that he hadn't climbed onto the bed, yet I could still feel him staring at me. I turned over to face him, and before me stood a figure---white gown, dark hair obscuring her face. I would've screamed had I had the ability to do so. She stood there, silent---but silent in a way that you felt a lump in your throat at the pain and the sadness that was radiating off of her. I opened my mouth to speak, but no words came. In an instant, she disappeared.

10

Sometimes just existing is hard enough, and today was going to be one of those days. Luckily, it was therapy day, so I could at least hash it out with my counselor. I had been so fired-up last night, digging into the graveyard's past, really putting my all into something. This morning though, I woke up, took the folded note out of my pants pocket from the day before, and just stared at it. What did it matter, anyway? Why was I so hyper-focused on this stuff? I felt numb and I ached to feel something. I folded the paper and dropped it on my bureau in the corner of the bedroom, by the window. I made my way through the master bedroom to the walk-in closet on the other side. Opening the door, I flipped on the light, walked in, and closed the door behind me. There was an audible 'click.' For a moment, I just stood there, my head pounding in waves as the quiet almost deafened me. I reached up, grabbed a small wooden box from the top shelf, and opened it. Inside there were a bunch of odds and ends that I'd become convinced were necessary to keep. At the bottom, I found what I was looking for. The blue box cutter. It is light in my hand, so light that it's almost weightless. I shifted the blade out and pulled the sleeve up on my left arm. Slowly, deliberately, I cut three incisions on my left wrist, to the side of the blue-green veins peeking out of my skin. The blood rises to the surface and fills the voids I created. The redness, the sticky warmth, the stinging pain, all collide to bring me back to the moment. I take a deep breath, place the blade back in the bottom of the box, and put the box back on the shelf. I go back into the bathroom and grab two bandages to cover the wound. It's strange how pain can be so comforting. Just a few slits on my arm, and bingo...feeling. I washed up, put the bandages on, and went downstairs for a quick coffee before I had to leave for therapy.

My therapist, Elizabeth, is a true 'nice lady.' She's a few years older than me, dresses conservatively, and speaks in a gentle and encouraging tone. I've been seeing her for three months now, but even so, I don't fully trust her. That's one of my issues, I guess. Trust. But then, there's so much more to it than that.

Her office was small but tidy, with the obligatory diplomas and bookcases filled with books with titles like *Healing Your Inner Child* and *Couples Therapy*. It had a large oak desk off to one side and an oversized chair facing the proverbial couch on the other side. I liked to think of the furniture set up as a Freudian joke, but I think it's more or less just the furniture that would be most comforting in the space she had. I often wondered if anyone actually lays down on the couch.

Our sessions are a bit of a cat and mouse game. Some days, I talk. Really *talk* about the stuff that's been bothering me. Other days, I talk about marriage or family problems, issues with the few friends that I have. Those are often the days that I most need to talk about the real problems, but I just can't seem to make myself do it.

We were talking about an issue I was having with a once-close friend, but the whole time, in my head, I was wondering if I should tell her about the woman. The ghost, or whatever it was. I do hallucinate, so maybe she's a new hallucination. I didn't know. I looked back up at Elizabeth and realized that she was asking me a question. Based on her body language, and the gist of what I was listening to, I faked an answer. She took it, but immediately asked another question.

"Sally Jane," she leaned forward and looked directly into my eyes, *"Where are you right now?"*

Her eyes were so honest that the sincerity of her question caused tears to well up in my eyes. I honestly didn't know how to answer. I blinked a thousand times and rubbed my hands over my face. I sat back, let out a sigh, and answered.

"I'm stuck."

She looked at me, encouraging more. She knows about Irene, so I started with her. Irene's reappearance in my life. I told her about the sleepless nights, the energy bursts, the depression. I told her about wanting to cut again but left out the fact that I had recently done it. Then I paused and took a deep breath.

"There's someone new. A woman, but…I don't know. I don't know if she's a hallucination or not?"

"What else do you think she could be?" she inquired as she jotted down notes.

"I don't know…maybe, I don't…maybe a ghost?" I felt ridiculous.

My therapist just nodded and continued to write.

"Have you seen many ghosts in your life?" she countered.

"Well, my parent's house was haunted. They saw a ghost. And I used to see a little boy, he lived on our stairs. My grandmother had visions, and they usually come true". I felt like I was defending myself in front of a grand jury. My palms were sweaty and my throat was closing up. I took a big drink from my coffee cup.

"So, your grandmother. She was psychic?"

"Well, I guess. I mean, she never called it that."

I kind of trailed off, letting the sentence hang there. Memories of my grandmother and her stories and her predictions washed over me. I squeezed my eyes shut to try to stop them. I missed her and thinking about her made me desolate.

"And you feel that maybe you might be a little...psychic?" she inquired in the same non-judgemental tone.

"I don't know. I see things, but then, I know I hallucinate. It's hard. I kind of find that stuff interesting, but I know it's not scientifically based."

"So it's not ok to believe in something that's not scientifically based?" she countered.

I swallowed and thought for a moment. "Well, no. There's God. I believe in God, and that's not scientifically based, I guess. It's just that psychic abilities...ghosts...that's more on the fringe."

"On the fringe?"

"Outside of normal."

Soon our time was up, which is always awkward. It's like, there you were, pouring your heart out to your dearest friend, then BAM, time to pay up and make another appointment. It always weirded me out.

11

Back in the car, I connected my phone via Bluetooth and selected one of my playlists. The sun was high in a cloudless sky and I was rounding the corner near the Walgreens when suddenly there was a woman on the road. I slammed on my brakes, trying hard not to shut my eyes. The car came to an abrupt stop. She stood there in the same white dress, arms by her side, palms forward, lips pursed. But it was her eyes that got me. She stared me down, making me feel like a child being scolded. There was an intense flame that burned in those eyes, drawing me to them like a moth to the flame.

It felt like hours, but I'm sure it was only a matter of seconds. She lifted her head, slowly, and for the first time, I saw her eyes. They were the deepest, darkest blue. A shocking contrast to her dark hair and pale skin. They looked like black holes that you could fall into and never be found. She looked incredibly sad. Her mouth opened as if she were going to speak. Then reality crashed back in with a horn blaring from behind. I looked in my rearview mirror to see a guy in a truck gesturing for me to move and glaring at me in frustration. I looked back at the road and the woman was gone.

That night, my husband woke me from a dream. I had been crying, sobbing to be exact. He held me close as my body shook and the tears streamed down my face. I was choking, I was crying so hard, but for the life of me, I didn't know why. It was in those early morning hours that I broke down. Between sobs, I tried to explain the deterioration of my mind, the hallucinations, the gravestone. Was I really going completely mad? I was questioning my very soul. Evan held me close and I dug my fingers into the small of his back, desperately clinging for reassurance.

"Maybe it's time that you go back to the hospital," he offered gently.

I scoffed. The hospital. The dumping ground for people like me. Shuffling around all day in no-skid socks. Doctors that are too busy to hear your problems. Nurses that are too overworked to pay attention to you unless you *were* a problem. Therapy classes that were a complete joke. People with good intentions gone to waste due to a lack of funding and staff.

"I don't think so. Not yet, not really. I just need to get through this, get my head around it. Please, not yet." The last was less of a plea to him, than a reassurance to myself.

He held me to him, and soon his breath was in that steady sleepful mode. I snuggled closer to him, watching the sun's rays make their way through our bedroom blinds. The day was beckoning, but I recoiled.

I called out of work that morning for the first time since starting that summer. Evan also opted to work from home so that he could care for me. I woke around midday to the comforting smells of grilled cheese and vegetable soup. My stomach rumbled as I stretched and rose from the bed. I grabbed my blue cardigan with the thumb hole worn through the sleeve. Wrapping it around me and sticking my thumb through the hole, I made my way downstairs to the kitchen.

"Morning, Sleepy-head," he said jokingly, "How are you feeling?"

I went to him, wrapping my arms around my safety net. I loved the smell of his cologne, with its fresh citrus notes and warm suede tones. I breathed him in and whispered, "OK." He held me tight for a moment and then pushed me back in order to look into my eyes.

"Are you sure you're OK?" his eyes filled with concern.

"I'm sure" I lied.

We sat in silence and ate our lunch. The world outside was proceeding as normal, the birds were chirping and the sun was shining, with or without me. I sipped the rich vegetable broth and felt it warm my body. The sandwich was extra cheesy and gooey and I dipped a triangle-shaped piece into my soup, savoring the mix of flavors.

"I've got to make a few calls and work on my presentation," Evan said, rising to bring his dishes to the sink. "If you need me, I'll be in the office". He walked over, kissed my forehead, and went off to do his work.

I finished my lunch, cleared my dishes, and headed for the couch. I grabbed a fleece blanket from the basket near the fireplace and snuggled down to watch Murder, She Wrote. It's my non-medicated medication. When I'm upset, watching that show calms me down. There's something about the simplicity of it that I find truly comforting. I pulled a blanket around me and snuggled down for some much needed TLC.

12

Later that night, I went to my messenger bag and dug through it for the slip of paper about the church cemetery. The woman I kept seeing was foremost on my mind. I popped open my laptop and Googled "Blessed Name Methodist Church Cemetery". Several hits came up, but one caught my attention immediately. It was a link to an old newspaper clipping of a funeral in the Monroe Journal. I clicked on the link and read on.

"Mrs. Jon Ashton was laid to rest yesterday in a quiet ceremony at Blessed Name Methodist Cemetery. She is survived by her husband, Jon Ashton, and their daughter."

. . .

I enlarged the piece and re-read the grainy text. I sat back and took a breath. Mrs. John Ashton. I had to know her first name. I Googled "John Ashton" and "Waxhaw, NC" and several contemporary persons filled my screen. I retyped my entry with the date of 1900. A shorter list cropped up, listing two John Ashton's. I assumed Father and Son. I searched Google again, adding "marriage records of" and hit the jackpot. There was a record for a John Ashton, married to a Lucy Schofield dated 1890. Another listed a John Ashton married to Mary Cosgrove in 1894. Mary Cosgrove. That had to be her. Considering the proximity of the dates, I deduced that it was indeed the same John Ashton in both cases, the first wife having most probably died in childbirth.

Suddenly, I was struck with a thought. I clicked back to the tab with the obituary. I backed out of the screen to the main screenshot of the newspaper. Scrolling to the top, I glanced at the screen searching for the date. November 13, 1896. Mary died shortly after her marriage. I sat back, feeling suddenly chilled. The hairs on the back of my neck pricked up and I felt a presence behind me like someone was looking over my shoulder. I whirled quickly around. Nobody was there.

. . .

In my dreams that night, I found myself back in the stairwell. The iron-rich smell of blood was thick in the air. I continued past the man as I had before. His eyes were wild and filled with terror. His hair was matted and clung to his head with sweat. At the landing on the top of the stairs, I stood facing three doors. One was partially opened. I could hear crying and gagging mingled with gentle murmuring beyond it. Stepping toward the door, I pushed it slightly open with my outstretched hands. On the floor was what I deduced to be a servant woman rubbing the back of a woman with long dark hair. The dark-haired woman was crying, her body shivering. I heard her vomit as the woman murmured in her ear and continued rubbing her back. Suddenly her back went still. Her arms straightened and she turned round to face me. Her eyes were filled with tears that fell against her pale, papery skin and her dull, matted dark hair. Her eyes blazed in my direction as she leaned toward me, arms outstretched, blood trickling from her chin.

"Help me..." she whispered.

. . .

I woke with a start to a darkened room. I had an iron taste in my mouth, and got out of bed, to walk to the bathroom. I flipped on the light and looked in the mirror. Opening my mouth, I saw a bright spot of red blood on my tongue. I must've bitten it during my dream. I rinsed my mouth and then climbed back into bed, the tear-stained eyes of that woman still haunting me.

13

I awoke the next morning with a sense of purpose. My body was buzzing with energy. My mania was creeping in. I enjoy these swings, where I can stay up for days and create and write and paint. My thinking has a clarity that words cannot explain and I feel in tune with everything and everyone in the universe. I had to be careful though, as these upswings inevitably crashed and burned. I decided to harness my energy, put it to use. There was no doubt in my mind that this woman was reaching out to me from the grave, begging me to help her. I just wasn't sure why.

At work, I couldn't wait for lunchtime. Gladys came in during the last part of the late morning rush, which occurs after story-time. It was the first time I didn't relish having a conversation. I tried to rush her along, giving non-committal answers to her questions and trying to steer her towards the checkout line. Once Gladys was taken care of, I punched out and went over to one of the back computers to do some more research.

My first thoughts were that this lady had been sick. Fragile and sick. Based on her clothing I remembered from the dream, I Googled "common ailments of the 1800s." It listed everything from childbirth and heart diseases to influenza to tuberculosis. I narrowed the search to include "bloody vomit", which limited my answers down to acute liver failure, cirrhosis, esophageal and stomach cancers, gastric erosions, and ulcers. I immediately crossed out acute liver failure and cirrhosis, since other articles had mentioned that many women in the 1890s were well versed in the evils of alcohol. That left childbirth or some kind of cancer, erosion, or ulcer. I sat back. Why would a spirit go through all this trouble? I felt that she was reaching out to me for a purpose, and it didn't feel like any of these causes. Nothing "clicked". I sat back in my chair and rubbed my eyes. My lunch break was nearly over and I was feeling defeated. I had felt sure that something would pop up and prick my brain as "the answer". Nothing though. I signed off the computer and went back to work.

I pulled a trolley up to the open side of the indoor return bin and began the tedious task of inspecting the books, checking them back in, and placing them on the trolley. There were two children's books with small rips that I repaired with clear tape and then noted the damage on the book jacket. One book had the tell-tale crinkled pages of water damage. I set it aside to be filed and noted, then stood up to walk the trolley with my rounds. I started in the Children's Area, filing away picture books and board books. The kids were busy coloring and building with Legos in the play area. Some of them smiled shyly at me, some of them came up to hug my legs. I patted several tiny heads and then crossed with my trolley to the Adult Section.

I replaced the history and reference books, the nonfiction, and the teen novels. I always saved the mystery novels for last, because I loved to look and see if there was anything I had missed reading. Stephen King, Tess Gerritsen, and Patricia Cornwell all went back to their rightful spots. A few Elizabeth George's that weighed a ton were shoe-horned back into too-tight spaces. Then I spotted a more tattered copy. *Lady In White* by Wilkie Collins. I hadn't read that in forever. It's a deliciously romantic story of a young man, a teacher, who falls in love with a woman who is betrothed to another man who is rich and powerful. The fiance fakes the death of his betrothed, killing a former lover by throwing her from the castle tower and then imprisons his betrothed in an asylum, drugged out on laudanum.

I stopped to think. Laudanum. Drugs. Poisons. I put the book haphazardly on the trolley and sprinted to the nearest computer. I Googled "vomiting blood and poisons."

The first poison that popped up was arsenic.

14

Thoughts of Mary now consumed my every waking moment. I read and re-read her obituary, so short and so void of feeling. I revisited my dreams, analyzing every detail I could remember. I was driving myself crazy, Googling her name and newspapers from the period, desperate for any information I could find on this woman. My shift at the library ended in the early afternoon and I decided to walk from the Library to downtown Waxhaw for a snack and to clear my head. I walked past the barbecue restaurant towards the local market in the center of town.

Provisions is a combination market and restaurant that serves breakfast and lunch and offers staples like pasta and spices. The food is amazing and the staff is super nice. The lunch counter at Provisions was busy busting out plates of piping hot food. I stood in line and ordered a grilled cheese sandwich and a cup of tomato soup. Their soup is the best, super creamy, with these wonderful cheddar croutons floating on top. I found a seat at a table in the adjoining room and waited for my food. The atmosphere is bright but relaxing and the walls are painted as chalkboards decorated with writing from local folks. It was a chance to sit and read and eat and think. And that's just what I needed.

I stared out the window at the passing cars and people, lost in my thoughts. I kept thinking back to my dream and Mary with blood dripping from her lips. She looked so frail, so helpless. My heart ached for her. My head started to buzz and I could feel reality slipping away. Through the window, across the streets by the tracks stood Mary. She was in a white nightgown with long hair so black that it was devoid of light, cascading down past her shoulders. Her dark blue eyes were set on mine, pleading with me. I could hear her thoughts. *Please. Help me.*

I suddenly saw flashes of her sitting outside under an oak tree on a blanket. A baby lay down by her side and she was leaning over, singing to it. The sky was bright blue and the sun's rays cast a slight shadow over the two through the branches. Then the shadow darkened. I watched Mary look up, her face contorting with terror. Suddenly the three o'clock train rushed by, blowing its whistle, bringing me out of my daydream. I shook my head and rubbed my eyes. Shit, I was going to be late getting back to the Library.

My head was pure chaos that night. I locked myself in my room and cried for a bit, then collected myself and headed back downstairs to fix dinner. By the time my husband got home, I had had it. I told him I needed some time to myself and went back to my room. I flopped down on the bed and just lay there, hanging on a thread between crying and numbness.

Evan greeted me with a kiss as I came down the stairs the next morning.

"Making smoothies" he smiled, "Would you like one?"

I nodded, still sleepy, and sat down at the kitchen table. The blender whirred to life and soon I was sipping a creamy strawberry smoothie. "Do you mind if I head downtown for a bit?" I asked, surprising myself with the thought.

"Sure, but why don't we go together?" he countered.

I smiled and nodded, finished my smoothie, and headed upstairs to get dressed.

15

Downtown Waxhaw was beautiful on that sunny Saturday morning. The Farmer's Market was set up on Church Street and we walked lazily through it, sampling cheeses and veggies with dip. I bought a small bag of dip mix and some lavender goat's milk soap. We headed further down Church Street towards the center of town. At Waxhaw United Methodist Church, we took a left to pass by Stewart's Village Gallery and then on to Crossroad's Coffee House to grab a couple of coffees. I loved the vibe of Crossroads, very eclectic. They have a fantastic collection of interesting coffee mugs hanging from the ceiling, and tie-dyed t-shirts and other small goods for sale. Their vanilla lattes are the absolute best, knocking Starbucks clear out of the competition.

Coffee in hand, Evan and I headed down towards Main Street. There's a lovely footbridge that crosses over the railway tracks between the two sides of the road. It's really a rush to stand up there as a train moves under and the view in either direction is breathtaking. Especially this time of year when the foliage changes. Trees surround both sides of the track, so it looks as if you're peering down a magic walkway. We walked up and over the bridge, pausing at the mid-way point to enjoy the view, then crossed the street at South Main Street BBQ and Frozen Gold Ice Cream. Besides the amazing barbecue, they also sell nitrogen frozen ice cream and a variety of mix-ins that allow you to create almost any flavor possible. It's my favorite treat on a summer day, super cold and really creamy.

We headed down the street, passing Maxwell's Tavern and the Gold Repair shop. About halfway down the street, we stopped in front of the Waxhaw Antique Mart. I told my husband that I wanted to go in for a minute and browse around. He rolled his eyes good-naturedly. My "for a minute" was usually at least a half-hour.

The shop was crowded but still had a "homey" feel to it. There were all kinds of antiques, from dolls and toys to kitchenware and records. I wandered up and down the aisles while Evan settled in the wartime memorabilia section. I love to meander through antique shops and thrift stores, the idea of touching objects that belonged to someone else, from another place and time excites me. I buy most of my clothing at thrift shops just for that reason. I get these tingly vibes off of the items, often with flashes of pictures of former owners or feelings of happiness or sadness. I walked into the store, going up and down the haphazardly stocked aisles, dragging my finger over toys and books, teacups and broaches.

I was about to turn to the back of the store when a table caught my eye. It was piled high with various knick-knacks and my curiosity drew me closer. I picked up some records and a few children's books. There were lace handkerchiefs folded and pressed and housed in plastic coverings. A large banana hook dangled with costume jewelry. To the back of the table was a small ceramic circular box. It was about 5 inches in diameter and had dark blue enamel with an ornate pink rose preserved beneath a sheath of glass rimmed with pearls on the cover. I picked it up, it was light and cool to the touch. I opened the lid and found a circular shaped indentation, opposite the small mirror in the lid, which must have been used for makeup powder. I clasped the lid shut and turned it over. There was a wind-up key. I turned it a few times then turned the box back over and opened the lid. The most beautifully haunting version of Minuet in G came out. The tune was lilting and light, but for some reason, it made me feel sad. I closed the lid and turned it over looking for a price. The tag read twenty dollars. I have a small collection of knick-knacks on my writing desk and thought this musical compact would fit right in. I found Evan and went to the register to make my purchase. The gray-haired, slender woman behind the counter smiled sweetly.

"Is this all, dear?" she inquired.

I nodded in reply. I could feel my face flushing pink. I felt like the whole store was watching me and listening to what I said.

"It's a beautiful piece," she continued on, "Victorian, I think".

"It is lovely," I said, faking a smile I didn't feel. "The music still plays."

She smiled as she wrapped my purchase in an old newspaper, placing it in a small brown bag.

"Come visit us again," she called after us.

"We will," I smiled, as we were headed out the door.

16

Back at home, I unwrapped the compact and set it down in the center of the old writing desk I had refurbished last summer. The desk was a 'right of passage' of sorts. It was the first piece of furniture I had "saved" from the junk pile at our local thrift store. When I brought it home, it had a broken drawer, some old cassette tapes in it, and the wood was chipped and stained like a bad tan. I sanded it down, nailed the drawer back together, and painted it bright white. I bought an old mahogany dining chair with a pretty patterned white cloth seat, and 'Voila', I had myself a writing desk. Since then I've tackled a few tables and some other odd chairs, but the desk is by far my favorite.

I stared at the compact and music box, running

my finger over the ring of smooth pearls. It really was a striking piece. I turned it over, wound the key, set it down, and opened the lid. The music drifted out, accompanied by the chirping birds from my open window. I leaned back in my chair, closed my eyes, and let the peacefulness wash over me. Suddenly, a cool breeze crossed the back of my neck and my eyes popped open. I glanced at the music box, and, reflected in the mirror in the lid of the box, there was a woman standing behind me. I quickly turned around, nobody was there. I looked at the mirror again and watched in horror as the figure opened her mouth and blood began to run down her chin to the front of her chest. The lilting music continued to play, sending an uneasy tingling sensation up my spine. I watched the spectacle unfold, mesmerized. I leaned in, toward the mirror, trying to get a better look at her. Her dark hair obscured most of her face and her arms hung loosely by her side.

I stared, frozen in space at the sight of the reflection. As I watched, she started to raise her arms towards me, and her eyes opened wide. Her mouth was moving, but I could not hear any sound. She was getting closer to me and now was at most an arm's length away from my chair.

Suddenly, the bedroom door slammed open, and

Finnegan, our golden retriever, bounded in tail wagging. He hurried over to me and buried his face in my lap. Finnegan wasn't just a family pet, he was also a therapy dog. He's trained to alert when I'm experiencing anxiety and uses his body to put pressure on mine to calm me down. I petted him and rewarded him for doing his job.

"Good boy! Good boy, thank you, Finnegan!" I cooed as he licked my face.

I looked back at the mirror on the desk. The woman was gone.

Focusing my attention back on Finnegan, I petted him and brought him downstairs for a well-deserved doggie treat.

While Finnegan was enjoying his reward, I stepped into the downstairs bathroom and splashed some water on my face. I patted it dry with the thick plum-colored hand towel that hung on the wall. I looked at myself in the mirror. I wanted so very badly to be happy. My face was worn and seemed to rest in a frowning position. My glossy brown hair was showing wisps of gray wiry hairs. It was such a beautiful day out and Evan and I had had such a perfect morning downtown. But, I could feel the depression encroaching. It feels like my body is disconnecting from my soul. A numbness enveloped my heart and clouded my mind. My body became useless to the workings of my brain, which was constantly sending out signals of negativity and the inability to complete the simplest of tasks. I desperately wanted to lay down and just sleep it all away.

17

Depression still clung to me like a wet t-shirt when I awoke Monday morning. The last thing I felt like doing was going to work, but I had already called out last week, so I took a deep breath and crawled out of bed. The shower was hot and soul-cleansing and I breathed in deeply, the scent of my rosemary-mint shampoo. I toweled off and looked at myself in the mirror. I looked forty-one today, every bit of it. The grays were peeking out from my dark brown hair and I looked defeated. It didn't take long for the voices to start in. *Fat. Ugly. Worthless. Kill yourself. Take all the pills. Take all the pills!*

With the voices still resonating in my head, I dressed and headed downstairs. We are all fighting silent battles that we keep hidden. It was still fairly dark, and that darkness just made me want to crawl back to my bed more. I fumbled with the coffee maker and made myself a mug. Grasping my hands around the warmth, I went out to the back porch. The blast of cold air woke me more than the coffee and I sipped the bittersweet warm liquid while I breathed in the freshness of nature. The trees were still wet from last evening's drizzle, and the dark colors of the bark really made the reds and golds of the leaves stand out in the haze of our outdoor lights. A few hearty birds were up and chirping, along with the nagging bark of the neighbor's dog. I finished my mug of coffee and took one last deep breath. Time to start the day.

At work, the outside bin was filled with Sunday's returns. The DVD bin was full too. It took me two cart-fulls to unload both bins and get them safely back into the library. Once inside, I set about the task of checking in each item and placing them on separate trolleys to be put back on the shelves. Computer Education Class takes place Monday mornings, so the library was packed with elderly folks on computers, Mr. Rickers buzzing in and around them, helping them figure out Google and Facebook and Email. He's a quiet man, with the patience of a saint. He not only runs the computer class but also runs the toddler story-time. Toddler's story-time is not for the faint of heart, and Mr. Rickers is a real trooper. He always gets them laughing and singing in a semi-coordinated manner by the end.

With all the books and DVDs placed on the appropriate trolleys, I plugged my earbuds into my iPhone and went to work. I listened to my folk-rock playlist, which generally calms me down and lets me relish the quieter side of my depression. I was in the middle of replacing the DVDs when I felt a tap on my shoulder. It was Gladys.

"Good Morning, Dear," she smiled, blue eyes sparkling. She was carrying an empty tote bag for her books and her glasses dangled around her neck on a pearl chain.

I took out my earbuds and dangled the wire around my neck in an odd homage to her swinging glasses. Gladys sways a bit as she stands, she says it's leftover from years of comforting her nieces and nephews as babies on her hips. "Damn things won't stop moving now," was what she told me.

"Hi Gladys Dear," I yawned, despite myself, "Sorry."

"Staying up late reading too many books, I see," Gladys observed.

I nodded, not wanting to explain the real reason I

was so tired. Gladys chatted away about the nuisance of the construction on Providence Road leading to downtown. She complained about the 10-minute wait she had to endure while the workers herded cars down makeshift one-way roads. I had sat in the same traffic that morning. It surely was a pain in the butt, because it was the only road leading to downtown.

I worked as she talked, Gladys, trailing behind me like a new puppy, yipping at my heels with her daily pleasantries. It's hard for me to feign interest when I'm depressed and the whole time I was just hoping that I was making the correct facial expressions for her corresponding tales. I was trying to listen, but my head was so foggy, it was nearly impossible.

Gladys chose three books from the cart as I was putting others away and stashed them in her bag. She walked with me until I finished my task, then I pushed the trolley back to the front desk with her in tow so that I could help her check out her books.

The front desk faces the glass doors that lead out to the front of the building. As I was checking out Gladys's books, I noticed a dark-haired figure run straight across the doors towards the bathroom. My skin prickled. The figure's hair was long and curly like the woman from my dreams. I hurriedly finished with Gladys, bid her good day, and rushed towards the bathrooms.

I stopped just outside the women's bathroom door to gather my composure. Slowly, I pushed the door open and it creaked and moaned in protest. I stuck my head in. Nobody was visible. I pushed the door the rest of the way open and went in. The bathroom seemed colder than normal, and I rubbed my arms through my sleeves to warm them. I walked forward, towards the mirrors and took a look at myself. Nobody was here. I was losing my mind. I glanced at my reflection, my eyes were tinged with red and there were dark circles underneath. My hair was in its usual ponytail, but the effect of the hair pulled off my face and the condition of my eyes and pale skin made me look like a zombie. I pulled a few tendrils of hair loose and let them frame my face. I closed my eyes. I could see the woman in my mind's eye, her hair cascading down around her shoulders, her brown eyes piercing and direct.

Suddenly a toilet flushed. I spun around to see a woman in sweatpants with long dark hair emerge from the bathroom. My heart was racing and I had to take a breath to calm down. Really, this was getting ridiculous. It was just one of the moms from the preschool storytime. I had to get a grip on myself.

Lunch came none-too-soon and I was happy to be off the floor and in the backroom. I wasn't very hungry, so I pulled out my journal to try to write. I started off doodling mindlessly, then tried to "journal" my feelings a bit as my therapist had suggested. Writing "I feel depressed" seemed way too cliche, so I jotted down words instead, in list form:

Dark

Alone

Scared

Numb

Pain

Nervous

Feeling everything

Feeling nothing

It made me feel a little better to see the words outside of me. I continued doodling, hoping for inspiration.

She wears a cloak

Woven of lies

She tries to tell

As not to cry

Scared, alone

She numbs the pain

Caught in life's

Relentless refrain

Not bad, certainly not the best poem I'd written, but I'd take it. It felt good to put feelings to paper and I felt my depression bow a bit in response to the glimmer of creative hope. I closed my book and put it back in my messenger bag, next to the soft pastels I keep with me just in case inspiration strikes. Feeling a bit better about myself, I finished the day on a slightly higher note and headed home.

18

Tuesday happened to be my day off this week, but of course, instead of resting and catching up on sleep, I decided to clean the house and catch up on the laundry. I had to keep my mind off of Mary. The whole idea was starting to spook me, in more ways than one. I was questioning my link to reality, whether my illness was getting to the point that I would need to go back to the hospital. Having Schizoaffective Disorder, I take several medications and attend therapy to keep my illness in check. The hallucinations are part of my life, part of what I deal with on a daily basis. But I still also had that ethereal side to me, the side that believed in ghosts and psychics and intuition. I truly believed that there could be a woman haunting me. Not many would agree with me, but I still felt it was a valid possibility. I did worry though. I worried a lot.

I worked dutifully all morning and by lunchtime, I felt I owed myself a break. I made myself a quick salad, with lettuce, carrots, cut up chicken from Monday night's dinner and some slices of avocado. I drizzled it with a little ranch dressing and sat on the couch. I turned on Netflix and found Midsomer Murders, a BBC show that plays usually on our local PBS station. I sat back to enjoy myself.

I was really getting into the story, so much so that at first I didn't notice it. A small black moth hovering just out of my line of vision. I turned my head to look at it and it disappeared. Great, just what I need. I thought to myself, hoisting my body up from the couch. I went to the closet to get the vacuum so that I could suck up the little intruder and get back to relaxing. I took the vacuum out, turned it on, and looked for my prey. It darted from the curtain, past the window, and then circled toward the TV. I watched it hover in front of the screen, then head for the light in the center of the ceiling. I extended the vacuum hose and lifted it toward the insect. It swooped left, away from where I was standing with the vacuum at the ready, and headed toward the far wall. I began to go after it when I noticed it go through the wall. It just vanished. I searched the room, jiggled the light with the tip of the vacuum, nothing. No moth. I turned off the vacuum and sat down. Where the hell did it go? I turned off the TV, walked the perimeter of the room, rustled the curtains. Nothing. The moth had headed toward the wall and disappeared into it. I shuddered. Usually, my hallucinations were not so...trivial. A black moth?

The house was stiflingly still. The air felt thick and heavy, like a humid day, except that it was October and the house was supposed to be cold. Suddenly I heard a faint tinkling sound. I stopped breathing to listen more closely. It was coming from upstairs. I stepped over the vacuum and rushed up to the landing on the second floor. The melody was coming from the room at the end of the hall, my bedroom. It got louder as I crept closer to the door. I reached out, and slowly turned the handle, quiet as though I was intent on not waking a sleeping baby. I peered into the room. The music box, that had been on my desk, was open and on the floor. I stepped toward it bent down to pick it up. As soon as I touched it, it stopped playing.

I looked around for her apparition. Nothing. The room was deathly quiet. I stood there, holding the music box, ears straining, eyes straining, heart beating quickly. A cool breeze passed across the back of my neck along with the slightest whisper of a woman crying. I remained still, closed my eyes, and willed her to talk with me. I waited. I concentrated as hard as I could, mentally trying to will my mind open to the possibilities. Then I had an idea.

It was a game that we had played as kids..."Bloody Mary". You were supposed to stand in the dark in front of a mirror and called out "Bloody Mary" three times, then she was supposed to appear. It struck me that maybe the same technique would work now. After all, I had just seen her in a mirror. Maybe if I turned on the music? I wound the music box key and then turned it over and opened the lid. I sat forward in my chair and peered into the tiny mirror. I let my vision go hazy like you used to have to do to see the hidden pictures in the geometric posters. The music rose and fell in time and my head began to swim. Suddenly, I saw a flicker in the mirror. A glimpse of a woman, in white, with her hair hanging in loose curls over her face. She began to raise her arms toward me.

"Mary?" I whispered.

In the mirror, the apparition flickered again and I saw the room from my dreams. The woman on the floor, retching, and moaning. Her sobbing and pleading sent chills down my spine. The vision flickered again and the mirror filled with crows, calling, diving, and darting. I sat back, too shocked to do anything. Then, I felt the room change, the heaviness of the air dissipated and the room fell back to reality. The sun was streaming through the bathroom window. She was gone.

19

"I feel like I failed her," I was crying, sobbing hysterically in my therapist's office. She was offering me tissues and reminding me to breathe deeply and relax. She often watched me come undone, waiting patiently for the moment when I would pull myself back together. I wiped my eyes with the tissue, the residue of my mascara staining the tissue black. We sat in silence, I with my head bowed in sorrow, she poised at the start of a question. It was Elizabeth that broke the silence.

"So, you think that this Mary, this apparition, is a real ghost?" she replied, playing Devil's Advocate.

The question hung in the air between us. I weighed my options. I could say "yes" and send us on the path of the paranormal, or I could say "no" and chalk her up to one of my many hallucinations. The latter would be easier, there's always more therapy, more medications to deal with such things. The former would be more difficult. Reality shows around the country were busily trying to prove or disprove the existence of the paranormal. There were no clear answers there.

"Yes," I sighed. I felt a mixture of relief and apprehension. I wasn't sure where she stood on the idea of ghosts.

"Ok," she began, "Let's deal with that statement. You believe that a woman from the past has been haunting you. And you believe that there is a reason behind the haunting...that she wants something from you?"

"I think so," I began, "I think I'm supposed to do something or understand something. I don't know. It just feels like she's expecting something from me."

"Well, what do you think she's expecting?"

"The things that I see---the blood, the sobbing, the dream---I feel like maybe she had unfinished business. Like she might have died before she was supposed to."

"Ok, ok. But I want you to rethink the word 'failure'. We've established that you really can't know what she wants---she hasn't spoken to you, correct?"

"Well, she said 'help me'. So I know she needs help."

"Help. Ok, how do you think you could go about helping a ghost?"

I filled her in on the research I had done so far, the obituary, the dates of her marriage and death being so close together. The dream of the woman vomiting blood, the gravestone that I found in the cemetery near my home. Elizabeth dutifully took notes while she waited for me to finish.

"So, Sally Jane, what do you think your next step should be?"

"More research" I answered without hesitation. Just saying the words was freeing. I felt that I had a path to follow now. "I could look into her Genealogy, find out if she has any living relatives. If maybe there's a story there."

"I think Genealogy is a good starting point," she replied, "but remember yourself. Before you contact any living relatives you may find, I want you to discuss it with me first."

I agreed and we ended the session. I had work to do.

20

Thursday turned out to be a beautiful day. The sun was out and it was warmer than usual. I gathered my laptop and went to the back porch. I sat down in the lounge chair and opened the computer. My home screen popped up, a background of a sunset with a gnarled old oak tree in the foreground, shot by me last Fall. I entered my password and went straight to Genealogy.com. It seemed simple enough. There was a small box at the bottom left marked for "surname, location, etc.". I entered "Mary Ashton, Waxhaw, North Carolina" and hit the search button. A new page popped up listing forums for people looking to make links in their family trees. There were 440,249 results. I almost did a spit take. That couldn't be right.

I returned to the search bar which was now at the

top of the page. There was a drop-down menu listing forum posts, forums, forum contributors, articles, and family tree maker content. I switched to articles and a shortlist of links popped up. I clicked on the links and found the marriage announcement and obituary that I had already seen. I went back to forum posts and clicked on the top entry with the name "Ashton". I skipped through the early entries, a headache already brewing from scanning so many dates and abbreviations. I read on, determined to find Mary Ashton. The entry continued:

Jonathan Nathaniel Ashton mar 1860 to Rose dau of David and Pauline Hughes. Jonathan Nathaniel II b 1864 to Jonathan and Rose Ashton. Richard Edmund b 1866 to Jonathan and Rose Ashton. Benjamin David b 1868 to Jonathan and Rose Ashton. Jonathan and Rose Ashton and Children move to Wisacky Area, NC 1870. Jonathan Nathaniel II mar 1890 to Lucy dau of Mark and Wendy Schofield. Richard Edmund mar 1890 to Judy dau of Eric and Maureen Vanderbilt. Benjamin David mar 1892 to Jessica dau of William and Patricia Wood. Lucy Schofield Ashton d 1892. Jonathan Nathaniel II mar 1894 to Mary dau of Thomas and Wilda Cosgrove. Amber Beth b 1894 to Richard and Jessica Ashton. Benjamin David II b 1895 to Benjamin and Jessica Ashton. Abigail Rose b 1895 to Jonathan and Mary

Ashton. Lucas Riley b 1895 to Benjamin and Jessica Ashton. Mary Cosgrove Ashton d 1896.

Mary Cosgrove Ashton. That had to be her, right there among the births and deaths of the Ashton Family listed in a cold, detached manner. People who once held importance, who once walked the streets I walk now, forgotten. It did strike me as odd that John Ashton had lost two wives in such close succession, but things were different then, and life expectancy was different as well. I felt such a sense of loneliness for Mary. I closed my computer and grabbed my coat and bag. I headed down to Harris Teeter and purchased a bouquet of sunflowers. I removed the cellophane wrap outside of the store and deposited it in the garbage can. Then I climbed into my car, setting the flowers on the seat next to me.

I parked the car in my driveway, grabbed the flowers, and started walking toward the cemetery. As I made my way up the hill and into the open field, I felt a manic sense of connection wave over me. The sun seemed brighter, the grass greener, the birds more distinct. I parted the grasses with my hands searching for the small marker. I finally found it and knelt down, placing the flowers on the ground before it.

"Mary?" I whispered, "Mary, I do hear you. My name is Sally Jane. I know there is something you're trying to tell me, believe me, I'm doing my best to listen. I just don't know where to go with it. I need your help. Please, please send me a sign that I am heading in the right direction. I want to help you."

The wind rustled the leaves and bent the grass to tickle my face. I stood up and took a deep relaxing breath. All I could do now was wait.

That night I had a dream of Mary, another woman, and a baby. She was offering the baby for me to hold, her arms outstretched, eyes frantic. I took the baby and rocked her in my arms. The child's eyes were so blue, so wide and innocent. They were mesmerizing. I looked back at Mary and she was leaning against the other woman, coughing and vomiting. I cuddled the baby, turned away from the scene before us, and sung her a lullaby. When I looked back, Mary was gone. All that remained was a crow on the windowsill.

21

I awoke with a purpose early Friday morning. I was sure the dream was a sign. I needed to look further into Mary's family tree. I needed to know if that woman that I had seen with her was her sister or a maid or whatever. I grabbed a cup of coffee and sat at the kitchen table. It was raining and a bit too cold to sit out on the porch. Sipping my hot beverage, I went back to Genealogy.com. I opened my notebook for the notes from the day before on the Ashton Family lineage. I found the entry about Mary. Her parents were Thomas and Wilda Cosgrove. I entered "Thomas Cosgrove, NC" into the search box and hit enter. Several forums popped up and I had to click through a few before I found the one for which I was looking. Thomas and Wilda Cosgrove did have another child. A daughter. Lydia Margaret, born in 1867. Mary had a sister. I followed the family tree almost all the way down, curious to see where it led. One of the names further down caught my eye. Gladys Victoria. Gladys. It couldn't be. I jotted down the names listed as Gladys's parents and the rest of the information about Mary and her sister. Suddenly, I was looking forward to going to work.

I got to work a half-hour early. I wanted to be sure I didn't miss Gladys on some off chance that she decided to come in before her usual 10 a.m. I tried to keep busy logging in books and putting away DVD's, but in reality, I was just watching the door for any sign of Gladys. True to her character, she arrived promptly at 10 a.m., a bag of books in hand, a big smile gracing her face. I practically ran over to her.

"Gladys! How are you? I see you have a lot of books to return, come on up to the counter and I'll check them in for you," I prattled on, taking her bag and leading the way.

She shuffled quickly after me, smiling and making pleasant small talk. I checked in her books and gave her back her canvas bag. She was idly chatting away, eyes smiling, telling me about the latest adventures of her grandniece and grandnephew. Gladys had married and her husband's last name was Fletcher. I was just hoping beyond hope that her middle and surnames were Victoria and Cosgrove.

Gladys asked after some new mystery novels that arrived, so I escorted her to the New Arrivals section and began the task of finding the titles on the shelves. I found the first two easily and handed them to Gladys for her to place in her bag. I needed to figure a way to broach the subject of her ancestry without seeming like a nosey parker. I decided on my approach and began to speak.

"Gladys, you know the neighborhood I moved into, Maybridge?"

"Of course, dear. Used to be farmland and a Methodist church if I remember correctly."

"Yes, well, I was walking through the neighborhood recently and I came across an abandoned cemetery in the center of the development. It's pretty overgrown. I didn't even realize that it was a cemetery at first until I tripped over a footstone."

Her eyes lit up, "Well, that is interesting!"

"Yes, I thought so too. So I was looking around at some of the gravestones and I have been sort of trying to compile a history of the people buried there. I came across a family...the Ashton's and they were linked to another Waxhaw family, the Cosgroves"

She smiled knowingly. "Of course, Dear. Ashton, I haven't heard that name spoken aloud in decades!

The Cosgroves and the Ashton's were wed through a...

"Mary Cosgrove?" I interrupted.

"Yes, I think that's right!" she smiled. "My middle name, Victoria, comes from that lineage. Oh, you'll simply have to take me to the cemetery! I'd love to see the stones and get some rubbings!"

"That sounds like a great idea" I answered earnestly, "It's up a bit of a steep path, but if we take our time, I'm sure you'll be fine."

"You know", she answered, "If you'd like to come over for tea sometime I know I must have some old documents and newspaper clippings from the time. Would you be interested in that, Dear?"

I almost jumped out of my shoes with excitement. "Yes, without a doubt, yes!!"

I finished finding the third book, feeling incredibly proud of myself and nearly bursting with the anticipation of sorting through whatever documents Gladys might possess. The woman was a virtual goldmine of history and I couldn't wait to get started. We approached the checkout counter and I spoke first.

"Gladys, I get off work at 1 o'clock on Tuesday. Would you be up for a walk to the cemetery then?" I didn't want to seem too overly enthusiastic about getting my hands on her documents. I wanted her to be the one to offer.

"Yes, that should work out perfectly", she answered, " should I meet you here?"

"Yes, we can take my car and then I can drive you back here. Don't forget your paper and crayons for the rubbings" I teased.

"Never travel without them" she winked, and with that, she disappeared out the door.

The rest of the day was really nothing more than a blur. I was too distracted by my newfound information. If Gladys was a descendant of Mary's sister, maybe she had some family memorabilia I could hunt through. Gladys was the type that saved everything, she had the Time Magazines from all the major world events, newspapers from 9/11, and I knew that she was a history buff, especially when it came to her hometown of Waxhaw. I was looking forward to talking with her. Maybe she could shed some light on the relationship between Mary and John.

I tossed and turned all night, anxious for morning to arrive. I just couldn't contain my excitement. My mind was racing with endless possibilities. I went down to the living-room around two a.m. to watch some television to try and relax. My whole body cried out for someone to connect with on this, and exhausted, I fell asleep on the couch sometime around 4 a.m. I was awoken by a kiss on the cheek from my husband as the first rays of light made their ways through the blinds.

"Morning, Beautiful," he breathed as he moved on to kiss my cheek. I leaned into him, eager for more. The skin on his face was rough where he hadn't shaved and his hands were strong and warm.

"Another late night?" he questioned, slipping his hand under my shirt. I nodded, skin tingling from his touch.

"Come back to bed," he teased, "I'll help you relax."

I smiled, leaning in to kiss him. I found his hand and intertwined my fingers, then we both rose from the couch and headed to the stairs. I needed to feel.

22

Whenever you have plans, the day always drags on. Such as it was with this Tuesday. I swear, I looked up at the clock at three different times and it still said "10 a.m.". I tried to keep myself busy, reshelving books, sending out late notices, and answering phones. Finally, the clock struck one, and like Cinderella, I was out the door.

Gladys was in the parking lot, emerging from her rusty blue 1994 Honda Accord, like a butterfly from its cocoon. She was wearing a plaid shirt and what looked like a fisherman's vest, with bits of paper peeking out from one of the pockets. She also had a camera around her neck and a pink visor on her head.

"Ready, Freddie!" she called from her spot in the lot.

"I'm the white caravan" I called out, walking towards her "Is there anything I can help you carry?"

"Nope, that's what the vest is for" she chuckled, "I must look like an out of season tourist!"

"You look fine" I assured her, "I'm really so excited that we're doing this!" More than she could possibly know.

We climbed into my car and headed toward my neighborhood. The signs for Maybridge started to pop up on the right side of the road. They were a deep red with gold lettering that complemented the red and gold leaves of the surrounding trees. We turned right onto Clayburn Street and followed it straight back to Deer Meadows Road. I turned right again and followed Screech Owl Road as it turned left down into the back part of the development. I pulled up alongside the curb where the trail could be seen leading into the woods.

"This is it", I proclaimed, pointing to the scraggly trail, "Let's go!"

I helped Gladys out of the car with care and we made our way to the start of the trail. I steadied her elbow, but she was surprisingly spritely at making her way through the weeds and roots. I asked her repeatedly if she needed to rest, but she declined. We reached the clearing in no time.

"Let me walk in front, Gladys", I instructed, "there are footstones buried here that are easy to trip over."

We walked a couple of hundred feet and found the first stone. It was a headstone with the name Hill etched at the top. The occupant's name was listed underneath. Gladys produced a thin sheet of paper from her vest pocket and unfolded it. She laid it gently over the stone and began to rub with a worn crayon. The words appeared on the paper like magic, and she smiled as she worked. It was rather a grim contradiction, smiling and having fun in a cemetery.

"Hey Gladys," I called, "Could I please borrow a piece of paper and crayon?"

"Sure, Dear" she replied, handing me the items.

I wandered away from where Gladys stood, completely transfixed by the larger stones around her. I needed to find Mary's stone. I parted the grasses, letting their tips tickle my fingers, constantly searching the ground for Mary's footstone. I finally found it. The sunflowers I had left were withered and dry, so I wiped them gently off to the side and stared at the stone. "M.A. 1870-1896" was all it read. My God, she was just twenty-two years old! A forgotten woman from a forgotten time. I searched in a radius around the stone for any sign that there had once been a more formal headstone. Nothing. Not even an indentation in the ground. I sighed. Could she have counted so little? Maybe her family was poor and that was all they could afford. Maybe teenagers had carried it off as some sort of morbid souvenir. I circled back to the stone, running my fingers over the cool, smooth granite. I took out the paper and laid it ceremoniously on top. Then, with gentle strokes, I brought her initials to life.

After I dropped Gladys back at the library to fetch her car, I headed home. My head was swimming and I was getting that dizzy feeling that meant a change in mood was eminent. At home, my daughter and her constant chatter were driving me crazy. Once the boys arrived home, I announced to my eldest that he was in charge for an hour while I went to lay down. Of course, that brought with it a new tidal wave of bickering, but I ignored them and headed for the sanctity of my bed.

My head barely hit the pillow and I was out. In my dream, I found myself wandering through a tangled forest. It was dark, but only from the inability of the sun to penetrate the canopy, not from the time of day. I could easily see sunshine filtering through the trees to the sides of the forest. I headed toward the light, it seemed the logical thing to do. I could feel the prickles from the brambles and bushes pulling at my clothing as though they were trying to draw me backward. I stumbled forward at the edge of the woods into a field. There was a wooden church at the top of the incline of the field, and I could see a small dirt road winding its way from the church down the slope and through the forest. To the left was a small gated cemetery. The sun was shining from behind the church, making it seem imposing and difficult to see at the same time. I made my way up the incline to a small wooden sign just to the right of the church stairs. On the sign were painted letters reading "Blessed Name Methodist Church". I ran my fingers over the words and turned to go up the stairs. They moaned slightly as I climbed and I held the railing for support. I held my hand out to turn the blackened knob, opening the door. The inside was just as plain as the outside. Lines of pews flanked each side of the room with a pulpit front and center at the far end of the building. Not knowing what else to do, I sat down.

The direction of the sun suddenly changed and it shone a brilliant orange through the far windows. I squinted in the light, shielding my eyes with my right hand. I paused for a second. I thought I saw movement just outside the glass. I waited for a moment.

Yes, there was definitely something out there. Something I wasn't sure I wanted to see.

I carefully stood up and walked slowly to the window. I shielded my eyes again and leaned into the window to get a better look. A woman with her back to me, her long dark hair blowing gently in the breeze. She was slowly waltzing through the waist-high grasses, her hands just barely brushing the tips of the amber waves as she passed, just as I had done in the cemetery earlier that day. I felt the need to go to her.

I turned and half ran to the back of the church. Opening the door, I sprinted down the steps and around to the right side of the church. There was an old oak tree about a yard in front of me, and the woman was just beyond that.

"Miss? Miss, wait, please!" I called a note of desperation in my plea.

The woman stopped waltzing and stood there for a moment. I stopped in my tracks, a few feet in front of the oak tree. She slowly turned to face me and a wave of recognition washed over me. It was Mary. Her dark eyes and dark hair. Her pale, clear skin. She was so beautiful, I gasped aloud.

She held out her arms and I thought she was inviting me forward, but a crow landed on her outstretched hand. Then another. And another. I noticed the tree above me was alive with crows and they all were headed toward Mary. She was surrounded. They were at her feet, on her shoulders, on her head, in her hair. A few were circling her with deep intensity. The noise was almost unbearable, their caws pounding into my head like a hammer to a nail. She stood still the entire time, her eyes pleading with me, her arms outstretched. The crows were a flurry of black now and I could barely see her. Her mouth was moving but I could not hear her voice. I stared intently at her, trying to make out the words. My eyes squinted and I concentrated on her face. Help me. She was saying "Help Me".

"I hear you!" I called out. And then I awoke.

I wrote the dream down immediately in my journal, as much of it as I could remember, while it was still fresh in my mind. I drew little crows and the tree and the church in black ink. I drew Mary, exactly as I saw her, arms outstretched. Then I sat back and thought. It had to mean something, the dream. The crows seemed significant. I grabbed my laptop from the floor beside my bed and popped it open. I clicked on Google and typed in "Dreams of Crows". I skimmed through the article. Adultery, narrow-mindedness, or concealing an evil deed. Concealing an evil deed. Somehow, that felt right. But I felt there was something I was missing. I read on as the article became less and less relevant then glanced over at my journal page. The swarming crows. A large group of crows. Wasn't that called a "murder"? I sat back and sighed, closing my eyes. I felt like I was finally on the right track.

23

I woke up in full-blown manic mode on Wednesday morning. Or, to put it more precisely, I never went to bed Tuesday evening and was buzzing with energy, cleaning everything around the house, starting paintings, writing notes, making voice memos so that I wouldn't forget a single one of my seemingly brilliant ideas. Around noontime, I took out my laptop and decided to map out what I really knew about Mary. From my dreams. I laughed aloud. I was writing a biography for a ghost.

She has appeared to me now about a half dozen times, either silent and sad or begging me to help her. She had some kind of sickness where she vomited blood. The sickness may be related to ulcers or consumption, or arsenic poisoning. She was from sometime around the late 1800s. She was young. She died two years after marrying John Ashton. She had a child. She appeared with a murder of crows.

Now, call me crazy, but this, to me, was adding up to a story. A mystery. Obviously, this Mary had some unfinished business or she couldn't pass on to the light or had some other paranormal problem. I seemed to be her go-to person. My grandmother could see visions and she often predicted deaths of family members and friends through dreams. Maybe I was a tad psychic? Hell, of course, I was a tad psychic. More than a tad maybe.

While the list helped in a way to organize my thoughts, it was just a list. I was no closer to solving any mysteries than I had been 10 minutes before. There had to be something more. The fact that Gladys was a descendant of Mary's family. That had to be my key. Maybe Gladys could shed some light on her family history. It was certainly no feat to get Gladys to talk about her family history, it was, however, going to be more difficult to keep her on my track. I decided to go down to the library and look up her phone number on her library file.

I jumped in my car, speeding down the winding roads to the library. I hope to God that there weren't any cops out because, in my state, I definitely shouldn't be driving. But I had to talk to Gladys. Today. Now. Faster than now. Stupid Lights.

I arrived at the library and breezed through the doors about as daintily as a tornado. Mr. Ricker's looked up and started to say something about it being my day off, but I just kept going. I got behind the desk and logged onto the computer. I pulled up Gladys's information. Phone number, good. I dialed from right there at the front desk. She answered on the third ring.

"Gladys?" I said into the receiver, "It's Sally Jane."

"Sally, Dear, how lovely to hear your voice. You sound winded" she said with concern.

I ignored that and continued on.

"Your family...the Cosgroves...do you have any information on them? Any newspapers, family bibles, pictures, anything?"

"Whoa, Dear, slow down. You sound like you're running a marathon"

This is no time for "Slow and Easy Southern" Gladys dear, I think to myself.

"Sorry, Gladys," I said, catching my breath, "I'm just over-excited I guess."

"That's OK, sweetie. Now, what did you want to know about?"

I took a slow, deep, cleansing breath and balled my fists to keep from screaming.

"The Cosgrove side of your family, Gladys. Do you know anything about them?"

"I'm sure I do" she replied. I sat back and let a wave of relief wash over me.

"Do you have time to talk to me about it soon...could you maybe today?"

"I was just about to have lunch. Why don't you come on over and we'll see what I have laying around"

I almost exploded with delight "Thank you, Gladys!! Thank you so much!! I'll be there in just a few minutes"

I hung up as she let out an exasperated "Oh, Dear", grabbed my keys and headed back to my car. Gladys's house was in the heart of Waxhaw, one of the older houses of the original settlers. It was a dusty blue with a wrap-around porch that was overgrown with Wisteria vines. If you didn't know better, you'd think it was abandoned.

I hopped up the two steps and rang the doorbell. I could hear shuffling deep inside and soon Gladys emerged, cracking the door. When she recognized me, she swung the door open wide and smiled.

"Come on in, sweetheart! I'll get us some sweet tea"

I followed Gladys into her home. It was like a museum. She had books piled everywhere, newspapers on a chair in the corner, knick-knacks adorned every shelf. She had several photo albums piled next to her easy chair and three cats intertwined themselves between us and the hoard. It smelled pleasant enough though. Like sweet tea and lavender, some of which I saw drying from the ceiling of her kitchen.

We sat at the kitchen table, an old pine farm table with benches on two sides and two chairs at either end. It looked well-loved.

"I used to host family parties here for the holidays," she said, with almost a whimsical sigh. She handed me a glass of sweet tea as I sat down on the bench, and she poured a glass for herself, choosing one of the chairs closest to me.

"If you don't mind me asking, Sally Jane, why all the interest in the Cosgroves?" she inquired.

"Well, remember the cemetery we went to? One of the graves belongs to Mary Ashton. She used to be Mary Cosgrove. I'm just fascinated by her, to be truthful. The fact that you share ties to her makes it even more interesting. I am really hoping you can give me some insight into the type of person she was. She was quite young when she died."

Gladys seemed to ponder this for a moment, took a sip of her tea, and placed it back on the table, leaving the two sandwiches she had made on their plates. "Ok, let's head up to the attic."

The attic to Gladys's house was actually an entire floor. We made our way up serpentine staircases behind creaky doors and the occasional cobweb. The room was impressive. At least the length of the entire house, with high ceilings and exposed rafters. There were trunks and armoires and boxes upon boxes of treasures. The tiny dust particles in the air glistened in the sun like glitter. It was a sight to behold. A sacred room. A magic room.

"Cosgrove," said Gladys, mainly to herself "Cosgrove...let me think."

I followed her around at a respectable distance pausing to run my finger over a dusty trunk or a stack of hardback books. I spotted her stash of older Time Magazine's, all in plastic sheets, piled atop an old dresser. She finally came to a stop by a trunk in the back corner of the room.

"I think this may be what you're looking for" she smiled.

I knelt down in front of the trunk. The Catholic girl in me rose up and I felt the urge to genuflect. I took a deep breath, unlocked the hinge, and raised the top. Inside were four period dresses, one blue, one purple, one black, and one gray. Underneath the garments were a few newspapers from the early 1890s, I put those to the side for later. There were some costume jewelry and a few religious artifacts. I started to open the tiny drawers built into the top of the trunk and found some handkerchiefs. The very next box I tried to open stuck a bit.

"Just give her a good pull, she won't break. Durable stuff that was" murmured Gladys.

I pulled a bit harder and the entire drawer came flying out, spilling its contents all over the floor. Letters. Oh My God, Letters! My hands were trembling. They were addressed to Mrs. Frederick Washington. The return address was that of Mrs. John Ashton. Mary. Mary had written these letters.

I sat back, overwhelmed. I almost started crying. I delicately picked up the letters, gingerly placing one on top of another as if they were made of the finest china.

"Can I..." I started.

"Please, I'm rather curious myself" replied Gladys. "But let's take them downstairs. The air up here is a bit stifling."

I carefully placed the garments and costume jewelry back in the trunk and closed the lid. Then gathering the newspapers and the precious letters, I followed Gladys back downstairs. We found ourselves back at the kitchen table. I put the papers in one pile and the letters in another.

"Which...?" I looked at her expectantly.

"The letters, dear! Of course the letters! Open them!"

My hands shook as I took the one with the oldest postmark. I gingerly folded open the yellowed pages while Gladys began to munch on her sandwich. The stationary was simple, a purple violet on the top surrounded by green leaves. I read each letter aloud.

24

October 10, 1894

Dearest Lydia,

The world is alive with color! I do think that October is simply the most beautiful month, don't you? The air is crisp and refreshing, the colors of the leaves pop out against the clear blue skies. I feel so alive! It's a shame that everything dies come November.

I've finished moving my things from Mother's house to my new home---our new home. John complained that I had too many trunks of clothing for such a young woman, but you know how I love my clothing! He is such a tease sometimes!

Our house is lovely, Lydia, you must come and visit me soon. It has four bedrooms and a working lavatory, a parlor, a proper dining room, a kitchen with a pantry, and a sitting room that dear John has claimed as his own. The grounds are lovely, there is a garden out back where I hope to spend my days sipping tea and lemonade!

It was such a blessing to have you by my side to bear witness to the love that John and I share. The silver heart bracelet that you gave me is such a fitting tribute to our love and our new life together! I shall wear it always and cherish it daily! John and I are excited beyond measure to begin our lives as husband and wife. My heart bursts with love for you and my dear husband John! I am quite simply the happiest woman alive!

Your loving Sister,
Mary

25

November 19, 1894

My Dearest Lydia,

I find myself in need of sisterly advice. I've already spoken with Mother, and she assures me that all marriages start off with a little bit of difficulty as the persons get acquainted with each other. Both you and Frederick have been married nearly four years now, and I look to you to calm my fears.

My dear John has begun to act in peculiar ways. Gone are many of our servants, those who served him and Lucy, save for Agnes, who arrives daily to help with the house duties, and a few farmhands who come to tend to the animals and the fields. John demands perfection in every way and insists that I lack discipline! I have been working my fingers to the bone, from sunrise to sunset, alongside Agnes. I dare not say it aloud, but I fear John has soured on me as of late. Where he used to shower me with gifts and kisses during our courting days, he is now demanding, and at times, cruel. Mother insists that it is the nature of a man to be hard, but John just does not seem himself.

On another note, it seems the mice are migrating inside. I happened upon them in the pantry the other morning. I must have John take care of the problem, I simply cannot abide by mice in my home! They frighten me!

Thank you in advance for any advice you can provide. I am eagerly awaiting your response!

Your Loving Sister,

Mary

26

December 15, 1894

Dearest Lydia,

The Christmas Season is nearly upon us. Have you responded to any holiday parties? John has not mentioned an invitation to any in our case, but I am still hopeful that we will attend at least one party. You will be at Mother's on Christmas Day, will you not? I know that you have your duties to Frederick's family as well, but I do hope to see you. Mother seems to want us to arrive in time for an early luncheon.

I have begun to decorate the house, but John has insisted that I keep it minimal and tasteful. How I miss the lavish Christmas decorations of our youth! A few sprigs of holly and a sparsely decorated tree hardly seem to hold the Christmas Spirit. I know I am sounding pitiful and whiny, but there is a reason, dear Sister.

I am afraid that I must burden you once again. I am most grateful for the advice you gave, though the thoughts and gestures you suggested fell silent upon John's deafened heart. I never know quite whom to expect when John arrives home. One day he is the kind and romantic man that I fell in love with, the next day he is cruel and as cold-hearted as a snake. I try to keep my heart open to love him, but he casts me away like so much rubbish. I want desperately to please him, but I know not how to accomplish this ever-increasing feat. This past week he shook me to my core, accusing me of killing Lucy! Lucy, who passed from consumption! I fear he believes me a witch of sorts, as he has certainly implied so! I know not from where these vicious lies are born, but they pierce my heart with such ferocity! His eyes were so dark, I scarcely knew it was John before me. I am shaking as I write this letter. I am at my wit's end, dear Sister! Please advise as soon as possible!

Your Loving Sister,

Mary

27

January 23, 1895

Dearest Lydia,

I apologize for the dire words of my previous letter, as it appears that happiness has returned to the Ashton household! All is right and perfect again! Your advice to be patient was true and God has answered my many prayers. John brought me the most beautiful painting from Charlotte yesterday! It is a picture of a vase of sunflowers--he said they reminded him of me, his eternal sunshine! I'm sure you will simply love it when you come to visit next. Oh, Lydia, my heart has melted once again! John and I sat and spoke for hours, just like sweethearts. I am simply too happy for words. My dear, sweet, John has returned!!

Your Loving Sister,
Mary

28

April 8, 1895

My Dearest Lydia,

Spring has arrived and the trees and flowers are blooming with fresh hope! I sat out in the garden yesterday, sipping my lemonade and watching the birds. We have a tremendous amount of crows on the property, and while they aren't the prettiest of birds, they do provide a fantastic distraction with their looping and diving in the air. John says the crows are so numerous because they seek the seeds of our crops and he absolutely despises them, but I find myself growing rather fond of the poor things. They do have such mesmerizing eyes, all shiny and black. Almost mystical.

I simply cannot wait to tell you any longer, dear Sister! God has blessed us! I am with child!! Dr. Yardley confirmed this as of last Wednesday. John is over the moon with delight, as am I. I thank you, dear Sister, for helping me to weather the storm. From now on it will be sunshine and rainbows!!

Your Loving Sister,

Mary

29

June 12, 1895

My Dearest Lydia,

I apologize for not writing in so long, but I have been on bed rest for nausea that accompanies my condition. Dr. Yardley has prescribed some medications for it, and they do seem to be helping. I have Agnes keep my window open on sunny days so that I can feel the fresh air and smell the roses outside my bedroom window. I do so miss being outside! Everything is so rich and so green and the garden is simply looking marvelous, thanks to Agnes. I just cannot wait to sit outside and enjoy the scenery.

How is young Frederick doing with his studies? I

hear that the first year of school is the most difficult for most children, but he must look so adorable in his pressed pants and shirt! Are the schools in Charlotte satisfactory? I'm sure you would not settle for less. Soon I will have a little one to concern my thoughts with as well! I hope you are well, dear Sister! Please write to me soon as I am tremendously bored!

Your Loving Sister,

Mary

30

July 9, 1895

My Dearest Lydia,

Thank you so much for your last letter! Your stories of Frederick and his antics left me in stitches! Charlotte sounds so glamorous, all of the shops that you can visit! All of the restaurants and theaters! I so want to go to the theater, I am hoping that John will take me once the baby is born!

Some of the farmhands procured some fireworks and set them off in the fields as I could not travel to the town for the parade. The loud noises made the baby squirm and jump inside my belly, it was truly a most unsettling feeling. The colors were beautiful though, and John and I sat in the garden watching them under the moonlight together. We had such a pleasant time.

Mother is looking to host a picnic here at our house at the end of the month. Please say that you can come! I look forward to seeing you and your family, as I miss you dearly!

Your Loving Sister,

Mary

31

I paused in my reading to look up at Gladys. She had a far-away look in her eyes as she sipped her tea. I went to open the next letter but noticed the date. It was from January.

"There seem to be some letters missing," I remarked to Gladys.

She snapped out of her daydream to face me. "That's entirely possible. Those letters have been stored away for years. I remember playing in those trunks as a child with my sister and cousins. Who knows what we may have inadvertently destroyed. It is fascinating though, isn't it? Sometimes I have to remind myself that what you are reading was written by a real person. It's easy to pretend it's a story or fairytale."

I nodded in agreement and opened the next letter.

32

January 23, 1896

My Dearest Lydia,

Our daughter was born on January 15th. She weighed 8 lbs 9 oz and was 21 inches long. She is so delicate and so pink, I can scarcely believe she is mine! We named her Abigail Rose, in part I think because of her rosy complexion! She is a quiet and thoughtful baby, her big brown eyes seem wise beyond their years. She has my dark curls and long lashes. I think John was initially disappointed that she was not a boy, but he seems to be coming around and checks on us when he arrives home from work in the evening. I haven't my strength back yet, as labor was intensive, but Dr. Yardley says that I should be back to myself again in a few weeks. Do you think that you could come and visit sometime soon? Maybe next month? I can't wait for you to meet her! I am tired, so I will keep this short, but I look forward to hearing from you.

Your Loving Sister,
Mary

33

March 14, 1896

Dearest Lydia,

It was so good of you to come and visit us and meet our dear, sweet Abigail! The blanket that you knitted is the perfect shade of lavender and I cannot thank you enough! John and I have spoken and we would love to ask that you and Frederick act as Godparents to little Abigail. Please say you will! It would mean so much to us both! I eagerly await your response!

Your Loving Sister,

Mary

34

May 23, 1896

Dearest Lydia,

Motherhood is such a trying ordeal! I scarcely have time to read or write, with the exception of when Agnes is caring for Abigail! I can hardly fathom how you were so energetic with Frederick! I am tired but still do my best to be a loving mother and wife! Mother has visited several times and sends her love to you as well!

John is such a doting husband and father! Today he brought me the most beautiful ceramic music box. The top has a dried pink rose under glass that is surrounded by tiny pearls. When you open the lid, it plays 'Minuet in G'. He thought that perhaps Abigail might enjoy the tune when she is with me as well.

How is young Frederick doing? I heard through Mother that he has had a touch of the fevers. Please know that I am praying for his speedy recovery to health!

Your Loving Sister,

Mary

35

June 4, 1896

Dearest Lydia,

Sister, I am beside myself! I had hoped that John was past his dark moments, but alas, they have returned! He speaks so often of Lucy that I am afraid he has forgotten who I am. I catch him looking at me strangely. It is merely a woman's intuition, but I fear that my beloved holds hate in his heart for me! He is so very cold and distant, I feel alone in our home. Save for you and Mother, I have no friends that come to call. Through it all though, Abigail continues to be my joy. She is now my only source of love and happiness.

Your Loving Sister,
Mary

36

September 28, 1896

Dearest Lydia,

Sweet Abigail is crawling and trying to steady herself on the furniture! She has the most adorable crawl, scooting along on her belly and pushing with her legs. She is a happy baby, easily distracted with toys, but she is full of energy! She rises early and goes to sleep late, so Agnes has taken to rising with her in the morning so that I can get some rest.

The past few months were so confusing, I was at a loss of what to write to you. John has returned to his loving self, I think, after months of ups and downs. I have a new confidant, however imprudent it might be. Agnes, although she is young, has taken to chatting with me during tea time. She has been a most sturdy shoulder to lean upon. And she is wise beyond her years. She was here when Lucy was alive, though her duties then were solely in the kitchen. She counsels me on John's moods and suggests ways I could improve my standing with him. She has suggested that we revive some of the habits that Lucy kept about the house, such as holding formal tea at 4 pm, drawing (which I am clearly not talented at), and playing the piano (which I am competent at). Agnes has been having tea with me daily now over which we have a polite conversation. I have found, though, that she is fiercely devoted to John, so I must curb some of my complaints less she tells him herself. But company comes so infrequently, that I have come to treasure our little tea parties.

I had complained to John about being weary, as it is getting increasingly more difficult to take care of Abigail as she seems to get into everything, and John agreed that a dose of tea every day was necessary to keep my energy up. John smiles at me more now, but he holds a peculiar look on his face that I find quite unsettling. It's almost as though he's about to laugh at some terrible joke. It's strange a strange feeling that I have, but I suppose it's mostly due to lack of rest. Love to you and your family!

Your Loving Sister,

Mary

37

October 21, 1896

Dearest Lydia,

I apologize for it being so long since I've written. I've taken ill as of late and my strength isn't what it should be. Agnes has taken over caring for Abigail, as I must lay in bed upon doctor's orders. The doctor has suggested that I might suffer from an ulcer, as my stomach is in constant discomfort and pain. I have no fever to speak of, but I tire easily and am quite nauseous. Agnes still insists upon serving tea each day to keep my strength and energy up, but quite frankly, I detest it. Please, if you can spare any time, please come and care for me. I need you, dear Sister, before it is too late. There is a crow outside my window now. I wish he could speed my message to you.

Your Loving Sister,
Mary

38

We both sat in silence for a moment. Mary seemed just so young and so very naive. There were no other letters after the one dated October 21, 1896. My only thought was that she must not have made it past the sickness. I sat for a moment, lost in thought. Gladys sipped her tea and reached over, patting my hand.

"Was that what you were looking for?" she asked softly.

"I...I think so," I stammered, "I'm just not sure what to make of it all yet. Do you mind if I borrow these for a bit? I want to reread them later once I've had time to think."

"Absolutely, Dear. Just take care of them. They are family after all" she winked.

We said our goodbyes at the door, and I promised to visit again soon. I actually meant it too, the old bird had a treasure trove of history in that house that I would love to get lost in.

The drive home was quiet and contemplative. I didn't even turn the radio on. I just kept thinking over and over about the letters, the dreams, the sightings. There had to be a connection I was missing. The letters made it sound like she died of an ulcer. Maybe I was way off base. I had to go through them again when my mind was clearer.

I let the letters sit for a day. I did not have a choice, really. My mood shifted and I found myself in the depths of depression. I muddled my way through work on Thursday, barely speaking, and wearing my headphones a lot. When I got home I went upstairs to draw a bath for myself. I turned on a podcast that I had only gotten half-way through listening to and settled back in the lavender bubbles. The day was a total loss and I went to bed early, right after dinner.

I felt slightly better at waking up today. I actually showered and made small talk with Evan. I sat at my desk, took the letters out the drawer, and stacked them in place. I tried to imagine Mary, a young woman with her whole life ahead of her. Marrying the man of her dreams, having a baby. But there still was an uneasy undertone to some of the letters. The changes in her husband. The quick decline of her health. I re-read each one carefully, mulling over the smallest of details. The part about John accusing Mary of killing Lucy struck a chord with me. Maybe her husband was unstable. After all, he had only recently lost his first wife, the seeming love of his life, and now he was married to a girl far younger than him. Mary seemed so eager to please. I imagined she dreamt of parties and servants and other happy times. Instead, she seemed to get a life of drudgery with bits of happiness scattered through. It must have been hard to understand, how John and Lucy had seemingly lived such a lavish lifestyle and she was relegated to Cinderella.

It bothered me how the tone of the letters changed over time. Almost as though she was suspicious of John, but she didn't really know it herself. I was suspicious of him, with his bursts of cruelty and then the gifts. The sudden and complete turnaround at the time of the baby. And those afternoon teas. Something bothered me about Agnes and those afternoon teas.

I read the letters and jotted notes as my eyes grew weary. I was getting a headache. Then I noticed something move out of the corner of my eye. I turned, expecting the dog, but it was her. Irene. The hallucination appeared when my symptoms were getting worse. I shut my eyes, counted to ten, then opened them again. She was still there, sitting curled up on the floor, staring at me with vicious eyes, naked body curled up on itself like a coiled snake. I could hear her whisper-like voice, in a teasing, sing-song manner.

Maybe Mary is me. Maybe Mary is me. Mary, Mary, quite contrary, maybe Mary is me.

I put my hands over my ears, keeping my eyes shut. No. This couldn't be. Not now. Mary was completely different from Irene. Irene had been around for years. She was a part of me. Mary was separated, wasn't she? She came when I wasn't symptomatic. I couldn't start unraveling now. Not now. Not when I was so close.

I stood up, turning my back on Irene and closing the door to her sing-songy voice. Mary was different, I kept telling myself. She wasn't a hallucination. She was a ghost. Oh God, I'm arguing with myself over whether I'm seeing ghosts or hallucinations. I went to my bag, took out a Valium, filled a glass with water, and swallowed it in one gulp.

39

I couldn't sleep the next night due to thoughts of Irene and Mary. What if I was just hallucinating this whole thing? Now I had dragged Gladys into it, I was going to go to the courts with my suspicions, it was becoming so real. Had I allowed myself to fall down the rabbit hole and come up thinking I was in reality?

Around 2 a.m. I went downstairs. I was just so frustrated. I opened my laptop and Googled "hallucinations", "ghosts", "paranormal visions", anything I could think of. Nothing gave me the answers I was looking for. Then one article mentioned the use of Ouija boards. I had heard that people thought there were dangers behind them, that they could open portals to the other side, that demons could attach themselves to you, pretty much everything they tell you in the paranormal television shows. But, on the other hand, I had used them at sleepovers when I was 12. Nothing had happened then----except the other girls moving the planchette to spell out the names of the boys they hoped would fall in love with them.

I Googled "ouija board" and clicked on the first link. The image of a simple ouija board filled my screen. I hit "print" and heard the printer come alive in the office. I ran to it, grabbed the paper off the tray, and went back to the kitchen for a shot glass. I sat down at the kitchen table and placed the shot glass upside down in the center of the paper where there was no writing. I was going to break another rule of the Ouija board---never use it alone. I closed my eyes, resting the tips of my pointer fingers on the edge of the glass. Then I waited. I took a deep breath and felt the hairs on the back of my neck prickle.

I leaned forward slightly in my chair and placed my two index and middle fingers lightly on top of the upside-down shot glass. I closed my eyes, took a deep breath, and whispered aloud, "Is there anybody there?"

I waited. Seconds went by, and then minutes. I was getting tired of holding my hands up. I whispered again "Is there anybody here who would like to speak to me?"

Another few seconds went by, then the shot glass jerked a little to the left. My heart started beating fast. It jerked again, stopped, then in one giant swoop, it slid to the top left of the board. I opened my eyes. The shot glass was directly over the word "yes".

I took my fingers off the glass and sat back to calm myself. Somebody was here with me. I sat forward, placed my fingers on the glass again, and closed my eyes. I whispered "Is this Mary?" and waited.

The glass jerked back and forth, but remained on "yes".

"Mary, are you the woman who has been visiting me?"

Again, the glass jerked back and forth and remained on "yes".

"Is there something you need me to help you with?"

The shot glass slid to the right and down. I opened my eyes. Slowly, it slid over the letters "R-A-T-S"

"You need help with rats? What kind of help with rats?" I was confused.

The shot glass slid again, this time over the letters "L-E-T-T-E- R-S"

"Are you talking about the letters that I found?"

The shot glass slid quickly to the word "yes".

"You want me to read the letters again? Is there

something important about rats?"

The shot glass jerked back and forth over the word "yes" again.

"Mary, did you die from a stomach ulcer?" I questioned.

The shot glass immediately shot to the right over the word "no".

"Can you tell me how you died?"

The shot glass began to swirl in manic loops over the paper, back and forth, back and forth. The sensation was so mesmerizing, I didn't hear my husband's footsteps on the stairs.

"Sally? What the hell are you doing?" he whispered harshly.

My head shot back and my eyes popped open. I turned to look at him, sure that my expression read the same as a puppy caught making a mess with the trash.

"Nothing" I blurted out, swiping the paper up in my hand and crinkling it into a ball in my fist. I stood up, helplessly placing the paper in the pocket of my dressing robe.

"It's the middle of the night for Christ's sake. Can't you sleep?" he strode towards me and stopped just short. Without waiting for an answer to his first question, he held out his hand "The thing in your pocket. Hand it to me, please."

I looked him in the eye, weighing my options. Realizing that I had none, I lowered my gaze and reached into the pocket of my dressing robe, retrieving the crumpled paper. Guiltily, I handed it over to him.

"What's this?" he mumbled to himself as he smoothed out the paper "An Ouija board? Seriously? What on Earth are you up to?"

Without realizing it, I had started to cry. I leaned into his chest and he reluctantly put his arms around me. My body shook as the waves of sadness poured over me.

"It's okay," he whispered, stroking my hair, "S.J., honey, it's okay."

I lifted my head and looked into his blue-green eyes. Everything was not okay. I was losing my mind. This time, I really was losing my mind.

"What is wrong with me?" I asked, breaking our embrace and walking to the counter for a tissue.

He let the question hang there.

"No really, Evan...I'm forty-one years old, it's the middle of the night, and I'm thinking that I'm talking to ghosts."

He tried not to laugh and held out his arm to me. "C'mon," he whispered, "let's just go to bed."

I took his hand and followed him up the stairs.

40

I awoke Monday morning with a start. Luckily, Evan hadn't questioned me any further about the incident the night before. I knew he wanted to, but sometimes he knew it was just better to let me be and to let me ride the thing out. It was only a reprieve, for I knew that I was going to have to let him know what was happening. I was going to need his help and support.

I had been dreaming that our home was covered in rats. That they were crawling over every inch of the house; over my bed, under the tables, over my feet as I stepped. My heart was beating wildly in my chest. I ran back to my desk and grabbed the letters. I began scanning through them and found what I was looking for. Rats. Mary had found rats in her pantry.

Suddenly everything fit, but I had to talk to Gladys first.

It was only 7 in the morning, too early for a social call to Gladys (even though I was sure she was up). I grabbed my coffee and went out to the back porch, wrapping my blue terry-cloth robe around me. I sat down in one of the chairs, curling my feet up under me so that they too would be covered by the robe. It was a brisk morning. My mind was racing with ideas. What if Mary's death was no accident? What if it was a homicide? She had written about rats. It was common to use arsenic to get rid of rats, especially back then. Her sudden regression in health after the start of the tea times. Did her husband poison her? The thought sent chills down my spine. How he could slowly and deliberately murder his wife, the mother of his young child. The woman that loved him.

I called Gladys at around 9 A.M. She greeted me warmly and was only too happy to have me visit once again. Evan was working from home that day. I think he was scared to leave me alone. I told him I had an errand to run, kissed him on the cheek, and went off to see Gladys. He was in the middle of an online meeting, so there was really nothing he could do about it. In no time, I was at Gladys's kitchen table, this time with a steaming mug of coffee in my hand. I decided it was time to come clean with her.

"Gladys, do you ever think about the spiritual side of life? You know, things like what happens when we die, Heaven, ghosts, things like that?"

"Ghosts, dear?" she mused.

"Yes, do you believe in them?" I inquired.

"Well, yes and no" she answered, "They said my grandmother had 'the gift'. That she was able to see signs of things that nobody else saw. She often foretold the deaths of family members and close friends. I'd heard her do it. But as for ghosts, I can't say that I've ever encountered one. Lord knows this house can be a bit creaky at night, but other than that..."

"Would you be surprised to learn that I do" I confessed, "That I do have a 'gift', that I do believe in ghosts?"

"Nope, wouldn't surprise me one bit, Sally. I always knew there was something special about you. It's your eyes. The way they look at me when you're talking. Like you're here, but also far away. It's mesmerizing."

"Gladys, I'm going to come clean with you. I wasn't just interested in the history of Mary. She's been visiting me. In my dreams, at night and during the day. She keeps asking for help. I think something terrible happened to her."

"Terrible, how?" asked Gladys.

"I believe that Mary was murdered." I went on to describe my dreams of a woman vomiting blood, of the murder of crows, of the countless times she's appeared to me asking for help. Gladys took it all in silently, staring at me wide-eyed. I wasn't sure if she was overwhelmed or thought I was crazy. I finished by tying in the letters---the sudden changes in her husband, the rats in the kitchen, the decline in her health after the tea. Then I sat back and waited for Gladys to speak.

"Well," she started "that is an interesting theory. It kind of makes sense. But how in the world are you going to prove it?"

"That's where you come in. I think the only way that we're going to know for sure if she was murdered is to exhume her body" I exhaled in one breath.

Gladys stared at me slack-jawed in silence.

"You see, I Googled "exhuming a body". I took my journal out of my bag and read it, "The courts frequently allow a change of burial place in order to enable people who were together during life to be buried together, such as husbands and wives, or family members. Disinterment for the purposes of reburial in a family plot acquired at a later date is generally authorized by law, particularly if the request is made by the surviving members of the decedent's family.

Disinterment may be allowed under certain circumstances, such as when a cemetery has been abandoned as a burial place or when it is condemned by the state by virtue of its Eminent Domain power for public improvement."

I paused, giving her a moment to digest the information.

"You are a surviving relative, Gladys. The cemetery is abandoned. We could have her moved for just that purpose. To your family's cemetery. It would mean going to court, but I'm willing to cover the expenses. As for proving murder, I read in several different scientific articles that arsenic can be stored in bone. I'm willing to pay for forensic testing of her bones to see if there is any arsenic present. Will you help me? Will you help Mary?"

She sat silently for a moment and we both just stared at each other. I felt she was on the verge of kicking me out, of telling me I was too crazy to deal with. Suddenly, the teapot whistled and I was snapped back to reality. Gladys stood up to tend to the kettle.

"Dear, I don't know. Getting involved in the courts. Digging up graves. All you have to go on are dreams, maybe visions. I don't think the dead should be disturbed."

My heart was crushed. "But she's already disturbed, Gladys. She's not at rest. She is clearly crying out. Please," I begged, "please let me help you help her!" My eyes shone with tears, I was crying. I hadn't realized until just then how emotionally invested I was in this project.

Gladys finished pouring the hot water in the mugs of tea, then went to the counter by the window to get me some tissues. She handed them to me, went back and retrieved the mugs, set one before me, then sat down holding her mug, staring at me for what seemed like an eternity.

Her eyes softened and she reached forward and patted my arm. "Girl, you sure have yourself in a tizzy. As I said, I'm not one for ghosts, but I do believe you when you say you're seeing something. Maybe you have a touch of what my Grandma had, bless her heart." She sighed. "On the other hand, you know I do love a good mystery. And one from my own family is hard to resist", she paused, looking at the ceiling for confirmation of her decision, "Ok, Dear. I'm in."

I jumped up and hugged her, startling the poor thing, and nearly knocking our steaming mugs over. I had to get home to tell my husband. This was finally going to be over.

41

Tuesday night I approached my husband with an outstretched glass of wine as he sat contentedly on the couch.

"Evan?" I whispered as I handed him the glass, "I have something to tell you."

He reached for the remote and turned down the sound on the television as he turned to face me. His eyes were full of concern as he looked at me expectantly.

"As you know," I began, "Things haven't been easy for me lately. I know I've been acting strangely, but there's a good reason. You see, there's this ghost..."

"Sally," he interrupted.

"Please, let me finish," I tried to speak over him, "there's this ghost. Her name is Mary and she's buried in the cemetery behind the house at the end of the road. I know it sounds fantastic, but she's real."

"She" countered Evan, "is a hallucination."

"No!" I spat rather angrily. "She's real. I've researched her and everything. She's even related to a woman I know down at the library. Everything matches up. She's real."

Evan looked down and took a sip of his wine, then set the glass on the table. He pushed his sleeves up above his elbows and leaned forward, placing his arms on his knees. He looked at the floor as he continued.

"Sally, are you off your meds? I think we should call Dr. Anderson. I think you should check into the hospital."

Dr. Anderson is my psychiatrist. I only see him for med checks every few months and to be admitted to the hospital. Tears crept into my eyes.

"No, Evan...please...I'm not that sick. I know this is hard to understand, but if you'd just listen..."

"I am listening. I do listen. And I see. And what I've seen lately has me worried. You're up all hours of the night. You write incessantly in that little book of yours. You spend almost all your free time on the computer or at the library. And what about the other night, when I found you in the kitchen in the dark? This is all adding up to a need to be in the hospital. I don't think you understand how unstable you seem."

Evan reached out and took my hand and rubbed it between his. I looked at our hands, intertwined, and started to cry.

"Please, you have to believe me. This woman...Mary...I think she was murdered. She needs my help. Gladys and I have it all figured out. We're going to have the body exhumed and tested for arsenic---we think she died of arsenic poisoning--- then she'll be reburied in Gladys's family plot. I only need about fifteen-hundred dollars..."

"Wait, what?! Exhuming bodies? Fifteen-hundred dollars?! Sally, I'm sorry but this really is insane. What on earth are you thinking?!" The force behind his words stung like a whip. I looked pointedly at my hands, tears streaming, then I took a deep breath and faced Evan.

"You aren't listening. I know I sound crazy, but I've never lied to you. This is REAL. I need to help her. Please, try to understand!" I pleaded.

"No Sally, this is just too much. I'm going to call Dr. Anderson in the morning." He spoke with a finality that I knew I wouldn't crack that night. He walked over to the corner cabinet in the kitchen and took out one of my many bottles of pills. He held it in his outstretched hand, looking pointedly at me. "Come take these, please", he pleaded.

I knew there was no changing his mind now. I felt

such resentment towards him, towards my illness, towards the whole situation. I grabbed a glass from the dish drainer by the sink and filled it halfway with water from the refrigerator dispenser. I then took the bottle of pills, dumped two in my hand, and without taking my eyes off of Evan, I swallowed them spitefully. Then I turned on my heels and went upstairs to bed.

When I awoke Wednesday morning, Evan was already gone. At first, I was upset, I had spent most of the night constructing conversations to convince him to hear me out, but in the end, I thought it was probably for the best. I didn't want to start the day fighting.

I headed to work after a quick shower. The library was bustling with people due to a homeschool group meeting and the usual chaos around storytime. I kept my nose down and my hands busy, sorting new books to be brought out for November 1st, and rooting out old books to be put into the "for sale" bin in the library foyer. I was still kind of fuming over my husband's inability to believe me. The more I thought about it though, the more I found myself seeing things from his point of view. What if he was right? What if this was nothing more than me being delusional? All I had to go on, really, were a series of coincidences. The fact that I'd found a name and a history, that could all be explained away by coincidence, couldn't it? Even Gladys, with her letters...maybe I was reading more into things than there really was.

Back at home, I apologized to Evan. I told him that I had had time to think about it, and I saw his point. He hugged me, then told me that Dr. Anderson had requested that I come in the next day to be seen so that we could rule out going to the hospital. I nodded quietly and buried my face in his shirt to hide my tears.

That night I had a terrible nightmare. I was in the hospital, in a room, and I was screaming. I kept telling the nurses to "help me help her" as I pointed to Mary, sitting on the floor, vomiting blood. The problem was, they couldn't see her. They approached me with a needle and two large male orderlies held me down as the injection pierced my skin.

My appointment with Dr. Anderson started at 9 A.M. I arrived with five minutes to spare at his second-floor office in Matthews. I greeted the receptionist, then sat down and waited to be called. I tried to distract myself by flipping through one of the many coffee table books "Awkward Family Photos". Man, and they think I have problems...

Dr. Anderson greeted me with a smile and ushered me into his office. After we got the usual pleasantries out of the way, he asked me about the events that occurred leading up to this meeting.

"Really, it's nothing. I just thought that I was...I don't know...a detective or something. My mind gets bored easily and takes me on these trips. I'm fine now, really." I tried to sound self-assured.

Dr. Anderson eyed me carefully. "So, this ghost that your husband told me about? That was just..."

"Just a figment of my imagination." I finished for him.

He shook his head and looked at me in a manner that gave me the impression that he wasn't sure whether he should believe me or not.

"Well, imagination is one thing", he looked at me quizzically, "Are you sure it wasn't a hallucination?"

I thought for a moment. She had seemed so real. "Well, maybe. I don't know. It could've been, I guess."

"Ok, just to make me feel better...how about we increase your antipsychotic by 5 mg? That's not a lot, but it should make a little difference if you are experiencing hallucinations. Deal?"

Our medication 'deals' had become something of a joke. I knew it was best for me to take the meds, but sometimes I would need extra time or preparations, like halving the dose or delaying the onset of treatment. It was one of the niceties that Dr.

Anderson afforded me in order to help me be compliant.

With my new prescription in hand, I left the office and got into my car. I stared at the small blue piece of paper then quietly whispered "Sorry, Mary" to nobody in particular.

42

Back at home, I phoned Gladys to discuss getting together. I know I had led both Evan and Dr. Andersonl to believe that Mary was just part of my imagination or a hallucination at best. But I still wasn't convinced. I needed to follow this through. We decided to meet at her house around 1 P.M. in order to go over my findings regarding the forms and to make the necessary phone calls to get the ball rolling.

I arrived about 10 minutes late to Gladys's house. My car had been almost out of gas and I had to stop and fill it or risk running out downtown. She had made turkey and cheese sandwiches with lettuce and tomato on whole-wheat bread. I sat down at the table as she poured me a cold glass of sweet tea to go with lunch.

"Let's eat first" she announced, sliding into the

seat diagonally from me. We both ate in silence for a while, then Gladys started chattering about town politics and the latest novel she was reading.

We finished and I helped Gladys clear the dishes. Then I opened my messenger bag and brought out my journal, flipping it to the relevant pages. I explained to Gladys what I had found out, about her being able to apply directly to the Chief Medical Examiner to have the body exhumed. I explained to her that all she had to say was that a family member was buried in an abandoned cemetery and that she would like the body exhumed and examined and then buried in a new family plot. She looked nervous like we were about to break a law.

"Gladys, this is all perfectly legal. Mary is a member of your family. You have every right to have her buried with the rest of your family at the Waxhaw Cemetery. I'll be right here with you if you get stuck" I said, as I reached out my hand and patted hers.

She managed a half-smile, patted my hand back, and walked to the kitchen telephone. It was one of those old 1990s slimline push-button phones, attached to the wall, with a long coiled cord between the receiver and the phone. She picked it up and slowly dialed the number.

Her eyes perked up when someone came on the

line. Suddenly, she pushed the phone in my direction, her hand over the mouthpiece.

"I can't..." she whispered.

I looked at her somberly and took the phone. "Yes, Good Afternoon. This is Sally Jane Riley, I am a friend of Gladys Fletcher. I am calling to find out about exhuming the body of a family member who is buried in an abandoned cemetery and having her moved to a family plot across town. Yes, I'll hold."

I twirled the phone cord nervously as I waited and began to pace back and forth. Gladys looked at me and I smiled at her encouragingly.

"Yes, Sally Jane Riley here, Sir. Yes, the deceased is a relative of a dear friend. The name is Mary Cosgrove Ashton. Yes, she's buried in an abandoned cemetery in the Maybridge neighborhood here in Waxhaw. Oh, you have? I see. Sure, we could come by on Friday. Yes, not a problem. I'll see you then. Thank you!"

I hung up the phone and smiled at Gladys. "He said that I'm not the first person to ask to have somebody moved from that cemetery. There's some paperwork that I have to fill out, but other than that, it shouldn't be a problem. We're going to his office on Friday at noon."

"That's great, I suppose," said Gladys, with considerable uncertainty.

"Are you going to be O.K. with this?" I asked with concern. "If you're not, really it's fine. I...I'm just trying to help..."

She nodded and we both gave each other a hug. I pulled back from her embrace and looked in her eyes.

"If you're sure you're alright with this, I could take a long lunch on Friday. Could you meet me at the Library at 11 A.M.?"

She smiled. "Yes dear, of course. I'm O.K.. I just feel like this is the beginning of the end, that's all."

I knew what she meant.

43

Gladys arrived promptly at eleven to the Library. I asked my boss permission to take an extended lunch and stay later for my shift and he said that was OK. We took my car and drove to Dr. Katz's office, which was located in Charlotte at the Mecklenburg County Medical Examiner's and Coroner's Office. We arrived pretty much on time and entered a large building filled with identical offices. We located the Medical Examiner's office and opened the door. The waiting room was sparse, with metal-edged leather seats lining the walls in all directions. A few end tables with lamps in the corners held outdated magazines about celebrities and sports and fine dining.

We approached the receptionist's window and I gave her Gladys's name. She looked at me with unnecessary disdain and handed us some forms. I would think you would have to be more of a 'people person' when you're working with people who've lost a loved one. We took the forms and headed to sit down.

I helped Gladys fill out the forms, as best as I could, and we brought them back to the secretary. She looked them over with an efficient glance and told us to take a seat again and the Doctor would be with us shortly. Then she slid the glass partition closed with cold, hollow, thud.

Waiting was the hardest part. We weren't there too long, but every minute seemed like an eternity. Finally, the doctor emerged from a wooden door to the left of the secretary's station and called Gladys's name. We both approached, explaining that I was a friend along for moral support. He glanced at me momentarily, then ushered us inside.

His office was an impressive collection of books, leather-bound chairs, a large oak desk, and several diplomas from prestigious schools. Gladys and I each took a seat across from him at the desk and settled in. Neither of us spoke.

"So, I gather you're here to inquire about the exhumation of a family member?" the doctor asked kindly. His white hair and gray-blue eyes were calming, like watching a rainy day.

"Yes, Sir," I answered, a little too quickly.

The doctor looked down over the paperwork we had filled out. "And she's currently in an abandoned cemetery?"

"Yes", Gladys answered meekly.

He didn't seem to hear her answer and continued on though as if he had just expected an affirmative answer.

"Yes, we've had a few of these recently. New developments popping up all over the place, families want their loved ones in the sacred ground. How soon were you looking to have this arranged?" he asked.

"As soon as possible", I interjected, "We already have a plot secured at the Waxhaw Cemetery."

"Perfect," he said, "I can have a team assembled and ready for next Wednesday. Does that work for you?"

We nodded in unison.

"Ok, well, if there isn't anything else..." he started.

"Well, Sir, there is one thing." I interrupted, "Gladys, my friend and I, we are history buffs and you see, and we found these letters concerning our family member. To make a long story short, would it be possible to test the body for poison...specifically arsenic?"

He stared at me for a moment and then seemed to ponder the question. "Well," he began, "that's all going to depend on the condition of the body. Hair and vitreous fluid from the eyes are the best tests, but I hardly see that being possible. Our only hope for any means of testing would be if we could find some bones intact and test the marrow inside. Even then, it might be a long shot."

"But it is possible?" I pressed.

"Technically, yes. Like I said, dependent on the condition of the body. Of course, the testing would result in additional fees"

"We're prepared for the fees..." I replied hastily.

He paused and looked straight at me. "Well, ok. Once we exhume the deceased, I'll let you know if the test will be possible" he finished.

Gladys and I looked at each other furtively, and then back to the doctor. We thanked him for his time and left the office.

That evening, at home, I decided to let Evan know what was going on. I'd gone directly against his wishes, and I knew he wasn't going to take things lightly.

"You what??!!" Evan hissed through clenched teeth.

"I went to the Medical Examiner's office. With Gladys. In order to discuss having Mary's body exhumed" I repeated.

"Really, Sally. This is too much. Do you have any idea what you've done?!"

I looked down at my hands. I had to convince him that all of this was necessary, or at least, not as bad as he thought. I took a deep breath and looked directly into Evan's eyes.

"Everything I've done is perfectly legal. Even if this all turns out to be nothing, at least Mary will be reunited with her family. That's worth it, right? For Gladys?"

"Gladys isn't looking at a fifteen-hundred dollar bill from the ME's office" Evan answered evenly.

"Right, I know. But I'll make it up to you. I promise. The wheels are already in motion. I know I'm right about this, honey. Please trust me." I looked at him pleadingly.

Evan rolled his eyes as he sat down on the couch. "You understand that I find this totally ridiculous, right? I mean, you've done some serious damage in the spending arena, but this really takes the cake."

"I know, and I'm sorry. But you haven't seen what I've seen. You haven't felt what I've felt. It's all so real, Evan. So terribly raw and real."

I sat next to him on the couch and he took my hand and kissed it gently. I leaned into him, nuzzling his shoulder. "I promise, everything will be alright."

44

Wednesday morning came with clouds and drizzle, as though the weather knew that the task ahead would be sad and mournful. I had Gladys meet me at my house so that we could walk up to the cemetery together to meet Dr. Katz and his crew. We both donned our raincoats and sturdy boots for the occasion. I took an umbrella with me, just in case, it decided to pour.

We made our way silently through the neighborhood. I think that we were both lost in thought. I couldn't believe that I was finally going to get an answer, one way or another, to the situation that had been plaguing me these past few months. I think Gladys was a bit more worried about the decency of the situation, unearthing a grave, disturbing the dead.

I glanced over at her as we walked and she was staring down at her boots.

We rounded the bend on Periwinkle Drive and made our way to the path past the last house on the street. The drizzle had made the path a little slippery, so I guided Gladys by the elbow, slowly, all the way up. The cemetery grasses were growing browner as the season bore on. The men from the Medical Examiner's office were gathered at the edge of the woods where the canopy offered a little refuge from the constant drizzle.

"Good Morning," called Dr. Katz as we approached, "If you could please join us here at the site." He was efficiently dressed in a white hazmat suit that zipped up to his neck. His hands were covered in sterile gloves. He looked at us expectantly.

I took Gladys's hand and walked steadily forward. The wet grasses stuck to our pants and boots, soaking my jeans through to the knees. You could see a small clearing where we had been last week, making rubbings of the grave markers. Suddenly, I found myself in front of Mary's stone. I knelt and pushed the grasses away to reveal the entire stone.

"Right here, Dr. Katz", I answered with a slight quiver in my voice.

"Ok, boys. Let's get to work!" He ordered his

men. They started digging with pointed shovels, heaving heavy wet slabs of grass and red-clay soil to the side. It took them about twenty minutes to hit the top of the coffin. Then came the more delicate tools to loosen the dirt around the coffin in order to hook the bottom and pull it out with thick ropes. I was afraid that it would crumble and fall apart, leaving a mess of scattered bones and broken boards. But the group knew what they were doing, and worked slowly and carefully, pulling the small plain pine box to the topside and laying it on the grass.

"The coffin seems to be in remarkable shape for its age. Barely any rotting," stated Dr. Katz into his voice recorder. He ordered his assistant to bring forward the coffin cart. It was a metal zig-zag contraption with wheels that could unfold to hold the entire coffin. The men gently lifted Mary's coffin, as dirt and rocks fell from the sides and bottom, and secured it on the cart. Then in a macabre procession, the assistants and Dr. Katz led us out of the woods, down the trail, and to the waiting hearse below.

I shook hands with the Doctor and he assured us he would have his secretary contact us regarding the testing once he had had the chance to examine the remains. We both thanked him and quietly turned toward home. I put my arms around Gladys's shoulders and she leaned into me. My eyes started to water, but the tears were obscured by the rain.

The next morning I found myself waking in a mixed state. I was partly manic, buzzing with energy and anticipation of the news to come, and I was partly depressed, wanting nothing more than to stay in bed and stare at the wall. Unfortunately, that was not a choice as I was already in danger of being late to work.

By the time I arrived at work, it was bustling with activity. I set about the monotonous march of tedious chores trying to keep my mind off of Mary. I tried to busy myself with the "behind the scenes" work, things like checking in books from the book bin and putting away DVDs. I wasn't in the mood to work the counter and pretend at pleasantries with the patrons. I put in my earphones and got lost in my playlist as I went mindlessly about my tasks. Lunch came and went and I kept checking my phone for any news from Gladys. Not a peep. By the end of the day my disappointment had turned into agitation and I was in a foul mood.

My husband had worked from home that day, so he was already there when I arrived home. He was in the middle of a conference call, so I quietly tiptoed past his office and went upstairs. I sat at my desk and pulled out my journal, writing down random words and phrases in a kind of patchwork poetry that I was trying to focus on in vain. I decided to write Mary a letter, to let her know, in at least a cosmic way, that I had done all that I could.

45

Dear Mary,

I've come to think of you as a friend. A friend in need. I'm so sorry I wasn't able to understand you at first, but I think that I've figured out that you need help in order to rest peacefully. My friend and your great-great-grandniece, Gladys Fletcher, have banded together to try to solve the mystery you set before us. As I'm sure you know, we have moved your remains. There is a doctor who can perform tests to help us figure out how and maybe why you died. I hope this is the path you were wanting me to take. We should know soon what the results of the tests are and maybe then you can finally rest in peace.

Sincerely,

Sally Jane

It was short and to the point and kind of helped ease some of my agitation. I went downstairs and my husband was done with his conference call. We met in the kitchen over cups of coffee. We discussed how I was doing, now that everything was "real". I confessed that I felt agitated and lost. I wanted answers now, but there was nothing I could do but wait. I felt Mary was waiting for answers, just at the edge of my consciousness.

46

Gladys called me at work on my lunch break to let me know that Dr. Katz had found a few bones that might be testable for arsenic. He would get back to us early next week. She then asked if I would attend Mary's burial with her once the body was released, and I assured her I would. I still had to get down to the Monument Center in Monroe to complete the task of creating a new headstone for Mary.

I left work at 1 pm and drove to Monroe Monument Center to meet with Bill who would be creating the stone. Bill was a kind older gentleman with calloused hands and brown, consoling eyes. This man had seen a lot of people through painful times in life and he did it with honesty and kindness. I chose a simple pattern for Mary's headstone: the Tree of Life, on a polished granite stone. I was going to have crows etched on it since I always seemed to see her with them, but it seemed too 'Edgar Allen Poe' and besides, the last time I had seen her, she was standing by a tree filled with crows, so I figured that the tree would suffice. We went over the sketches one last time and he promised to have it ready for me by next Tuesday.

I drove home feeling a mixture of satisfaction and grief. I had crossed one more thing off my list of "things to do", but it was a sad errand and it was making me realize the finality of what we were doing. We were laying a woman to rest. A woman who, for some reason, had passed away at a young age and was restlessly wandering this world in the afterlife. I wanted to give her peace. I wanted to give her a place to finally rest.

The rest of the afternoon went pretty simply. I finished a poem that had been sitting half-naked in my notebook for weeks. I started a mixed-media piece and really wasn't sure where I was going with it. After a while, it felt like I was just layering paint and paper to go through the motions, so I stopped and went in to start dinner.

It was Halloween night. Our neighborhood is fantastic if you're a kid. Lots of neighbors giving out lots of treats. We kept our light on for almost three hours, children with their pillowcase candy bags starting to drag on the pavement with their effort to hoist their loot. By 8 o'clock, I was ready to call it a night, and I was getting tired of obnoxious teenagers. It was then that I noticed I had a missed call on my phone. Gladys.

I called her back immediately, hoping she wasn't already in bed. She answered on the first ring.

"Hi Gladys, it's me, Sally Jane. Sorry I missed your call."

"Oh, Sally! I'm so glad it's you. Did you get my message?"

"Ummm...sorry, no. I just saw your number and dialed you back."

"Dr. Katz called this afternoon. He said he doesn't usually work weekends, but he had stopped by the office to collect some files and there was a delivery on the doorstep from FedEx. He opened it and it was the results of the testing on Mary."

I held my breath.

"You still there, honey?" called Gladys.

"Yes, I'm still here," I answered, "What...what did the results say?"

"Are you sitting down dear?" she asked concernedly.

I lied that I was.

"They were able to test some of the bones from her legs and upper arms. I forgot what the names were that he said. But some had just the tiniest amount of marrow left. He said that's what they used to test with, the marrow."

"And?" I asked in a tiny voice, my throat felt like it was closing up.

"You were right, Dear. Arsenic. A considerable amount he said, considering the age of the specimen. You were right Sally Jane. Mary died of arsenic poisoning."

I slid my back against the wall and sat on the floor. I didn't know what to say. Tears started to stream down my cheeks and my voice cracked when I answered her.

"Thank you, Gladys. Thank you for telling me. I'll talk to you tomorrow".

I hung up and went to find my husband. I fell into his arms, tears streaming, trying to explain the news through choking sobs. He held me tightly and whispered that things were going to be alright. That I had done well. Now Mary could find rest.

I told him I had something to do. I grabbed a flashlight and went up to the old cemetery. It was dark and the moon shone through the trees. I walked over to her now open gravesite and shone the flashlight on it and over the old footstone.

"Mary," I whispered, "I know you're gone from

here now, but if you can hear me, we know. We know."

The wind picked up and rustled the leaves in the tree, blowing the grasses like the sea. I breathed in the cool fresh air and turned for home.

47

Gladys and I stood side by side dressed in black at the open gravesite. Mary's new white coffin was closed, suspended above the hole, with a bouquet of fresh roses on top. A priest was standing at the head of the coffin, saying prayers and giving blessings. When he finished, he asked if I would like to share a few words. I stepped forward.

"Mary, you have been a force in my life. I am grateful that you chose me to help you. I am grateful for the opportunity to know you, even just a little bit. I feel like you are my friend and I hope that you know that you will not be forgotten. I'm sorry about your death, I wish there were something we could do about it today, but those days are long passed. Know that your secret has been unearthed and that you can now rest in peace knowing that we know of the wrong you were dealt. Hopefully, now you can find peace and light and finally be at rest."

Gladys squeezed my hand and we both bowed our heads as they lowered the casket into the ground. The sun was shining high in the sky and the wind was gently swaying the trees. Suddenly I heard the caw of a crow overhead and looked up. Across the cemetery, I saw her, just beyond a bench by an old oak tree. Mary. She was standing in a light blue dress, hair cascading down her shoulders, eyes dark and playful. There was a smile on her lips. I turned to get Gladys's attention, but she had already disappeared.

AFTERWORD

Mary enjoyed the quiet just before dawn, before the birds awoke and while the moon still hung low in the sky. She would slide silently from her marriage bed, and slip through the bedroom and down the stairs into the kitchen to light the woodstove. The crackle of the fire and the dancing flames mesmerized her, the way they reached heavenward, almost as though they were trying desperately to take flight and escape through the flue. To get away. To leave their earthly prison and fly away to freedom.

John lay sleeping in the room above. He was not a terrible man, just not the man she thought he was when she married him. He had been such an adoring suitor, bringing her wildflowers, taking her on long walks at sunset, stealing kisses when they were sure no one was the wiser. John was several years older than Mary. Fifteen to be exact. And he had been married before. To Lucy. Lucy had been a kind and beautiful, fragile, woman. Mary had often seen her about town and at church. She would have had beautiful children. But God didn't bless her in that way.

Lucy passed away two years ago when the consumption epidemic passed through their town. Her funeral had been elaborate---horse-drawn carriage draped in white lilies, a solitary violin at the gravesite played a mournful tune---practically the whole town had been in attendance. It seems sacrilegious, but it was at the funeral that Mary first noticed John. And he, her. He had been standing, stoic, but teary-eyed at the gravesite. His hands clasped in front, fervently rubbing together, eyes cast downward, but at one poignant moment, he raised his eyes and they caught hers. They held each other's gaze for a moment and a warmth spread over her that she had never felt when any other man had looked her way. It was Mary that broke the spell. It was Mary that looked away first.

A few months later, John approached her after Sunday service. Just small talk, the weather, the sermon. He stood close, but not too close as to arise suspicion. He asked her if she might like to join him for a walk the following Saturday. Down by the lake.

They could feed the ducks. Mary had accepted. John was a handsome and successful man.

Their courtship had been the stuff of fairy-tales. John doted on Mary, buying her gifts and writing her poetry. It was the poetry that was her favorite. She still kept all of them, hidden away in her writing desk drawer. Though now, when she read them, she felt sorrow.

Mary and John had been married in a quiet cere-mony in October at the church with a few close friends and family. Her sister Lydia had been the Maid of Honor. It was romantic, she had thought at the time, but those thoughts were soon quelled with feelings of jealousy as the town folk compared her quaint event to the lavish ceremony that John and Lucy had enjoyed.

But John loved her, he told her so. It used to be every day, but lately, not so often. He was quiet now, sullen and prone to fits of anger over the slightest things. Mary found herself dreading their time together, never knowing which way his mood would swing. Would he be the charming prince that won her heart, or the violent monster that she was sure was getting ever closer to physically striking her?

She crossed the kitchen from the woodstove to the cupboards and took out the flour, sugar, and yeast. She hastily mixed and then lay towels over the bowl for the bread to rise. Next, she grabbed her cloak and walked out into the cool morning air, still dark, still damp with the evening's tears, and removed some eggs from the chicken coop, letting the silly birds out into the yard to forage and frolic. Lastly, she walked to the barn to let out the horses and give the cow a milking for their breakfast. The servants would be arriving from town soon to do the real laboring. John was strictly against having others live in their home, not even a maid. He liked his privacy.

Mary was out hanging the wash with the maid when her husband approached. "I've got to head into town on business," he said, leaning in to kiss her cheek. She lived for those little tokens of affection. So very often he was cold and distant. They had been trying for a baby and she had yet to conceive. She prayed nightly, to the Blessed Virgin Mary, because she felt that Mary would understand. That Mary would ease the pain in her heart, will her womb to be fruitful. If John knew that she prayed to any religious figure other than God himself, he'd beat her for sure. Mother Mary was her secret, a secret she kept deep in her heart.

> *Hail Mary,*
> *Full of Grace,*
> *The Lord be with Thee*

Blessed art Thou
Amongst women
And Blessed is the fruit of thy womb, Jesus
Holy Mary
Mother of God
Pray for us sinners
Now and at the hour of our death
Amen

It was dark before John returned again. Mary's skin prickled as though a cold breeze had blown through as he passed her in the parlor room where she was reading by the flickering light of the lantern. She could smell the booze on his breath, smell the tobacco smoke from the bar he had been to. Suddenly, despite the late hour and her tired mind, her whole body went on alert. She could hear him pulling things from the cabinets and the larder and smacking them on the tabletops. He was talking but mumbling, and she couldn't be certain of what he was saying. She stood, debating on heading to bed or further into the kitchen to help him. Then he called to her.

His voice was sweet but filled with underlying malice. Mary willed herself to go to her husband. He was cutting into an apple and pulling the sweet flesh off of the paring knife and into his mouth. She watched him, mesmerized.

"Mary, Mary, Mary" he chanted, in almost a sing-song voice, "Mistress, Mary quite contrary"

She stood her ground, looking past him at the wall behind.

"How'd you do it, sweetheart? My sweet little devil?"

Mary was at a loss. Sometimes John spoke in riddles, especially when he was agitated, which he clearly was. She wasn't sure if it was better to answer or remain silent.

"I'm talking to you, Mary," he drawled her name out. "Tell me how you did it"

"John, I'm--I'm not sure what you're speaking of"

"Lucy. How did you kill her, you little devil? I know it was you. I know." John spat the words out like a bitter ale.

Before she knew what was happening, he had grabbed her wrist and pulled her to him. She tried to push off him with her other hand, but he grasped that as well and looked down at her, eyes wild and devilish.

"John, Lucy died of consumption. Nobody killed her. I didn't kill her. Please, John, please let me be."

She searched his eyes for sympathy but found only repulsion. He held her wrists tighter, practically lifting her off the floor. She winced in pain, but that seemed to only fuel his anger.

"You think that is pain? You think that hurts? What about poor Lucy? The pain she endured? The sickness? You have no idea of pain woman. But you will."

He let her go and abruptly turned out of the room. Mary finally caught her breath and started to sob. Feeling alone and frightened, she ran up the stairs to the guest bedroom and locked the door. Exhausted, she lay down on the bed and sobbed.

Mary roused herself at dawn, her body stiff and achy from her fitful sleep. She tended to the wood-stove and then went to grab a cloak from her bedroom to go outside and start the chores in the barn. She figured John would still be asleep. He wasn't.

She felt his eyes on her back as she reached for the hook that held her cloak.

"Mary, I love you," he whispered.

The words stung like a thousand bees, for his love was hurtful. She choked back some tears and whispered back.

"I love you too, husband".

With that, she took her cloak, and walked out to the barn, tears streaming down her cheeks.

John stayed home that day, working at his large,

cherry, writing desk in the sitting room. It was really the only sitting room in the house, but he claimed it, and nobody was allowed inside. The parlor they used as a formal sitting room for guests, and of course, there was the formal dining room which they used when friends came to call. Friends didn't come to call so often anymore.

Mary busied herself with mending clothes and washing dishes. She did her work alongside the servants as they scrubbed and mopped. Most "ladies of the house" wouldn't dare be caught doing such drudgery, but John had insisted. He told her it would build character. That she lacked discipline. That was the first time he had spoken harshly toward her. It had been the second day of their marriage.

Mary went to the pantry to gather some flour and sugar for scones she would be making for tea time. As she entered the pantry, several mice scattered in different directions, causing her to step back and shriek. No matter how common rodents were on their small farm, she just couldn't get used to them. And she wouldn't abide them in her kitchen. She made a mental note to ask John to pick up some poison the next time he was in town.

John strode into the dining room area around noon time for his meal, sat at the table, and waited to be served. Potatoes, some leftover roast, and carrots.

It was mostly root vegetables this time of year. Their eyes met as she set his plate before him.

"Dine with me, Mary".

She fetched a small plate for herself and sat down at the far end of the table, across from him. They both ate in silence, only the scurrying of the house-maid broke the quiet. He dismissed the maid from the room and addressed Mary.

"Did I ever tell you, Mary, how Lucy and I met?" She nodded. He had, a thousand times since their marriage. It had been at a church supper, and she had dropped her plate, and he gallantly came to her rescue and fetched her a new one. Their connection was instant, their courtship intense. Mary always listened to the stories of Lucy with a smile on her face, even while her heart was breaking.

"I remember seeing you, Mary, at Church, and at the Markets. Watching us. How you envied our love. I could see it plainly on your face"

Mary was taken aback. She couldn't remember a single time she had interacted with Lucy and John. Oh, she knew about them, knew them well enough to wave "Hello", but that was it. And she most certainly had never stared at them. She began to get that queasy feeling in the pit of her stomach and could feel tiny beads of sweat form on her upper lip. She wanted to jump up from the table and run, out into the fields, out into the forest---anywhere but here. Instead, she sat. And waited.

John pushed his chair back and stood up. He walked slowly toward Mary, dragging his finger along the wooden table, his eyes never leaving hers. Mary tried to swallow but her mouth was too dry. Her hands shook as she reached for her water and took the smallest of sips.

As soon as she put down the glass, he grabbed her wrist. Twisted her arm so that she had to look directly up at him.

"You envied my Lucy, didn't you, Mary? You envied her and wanted me. And like a fool, I fell for it. I fell under your spell. How, Mary? How did you kill her you, little witch? Demons? Do you command Demons?" He spat as he spoke, he was so angry.

Mary whimpered, "I am not a witch, John. I love you. I loved Lucy. I would never have hurt her. I have no Demons, no Demons, John! I swear, I love you. I love you!" She started to weep.

John let go of her wrist, turned on his heel, and walked out of the room. She could hear the door to the sitting room slam shut. She rubbed her wrist and cried.

Mary composed herself and went to the kitchen, carrying the barely touched lunch plates with her. The maid was cleaning the breakfast dishes. Mary told her that she was going to take the carriage into town and go to the market and the butchery. She grabbed a basket from the peg in the closet and wrapped her cloak around her shoulders. Finley, one of the farmhands, waved as she approached the barn. She told him of her wishes and he readied the carriage. With the horses hitched, he helped her gently into the cab and moved to the front to take the reigns. The carriage started forward with a jolt as the horses began to canter. Mary steadied herself against the inside of the cab as it bobbed up and down from the potholes in the road.

Finley stopped the carriage in the center of town and helped Mary out. She told him she would be going to the market and the butcher shop and to meet her at the south end of Main street in approximately an hour to pick her up.

The day was cool but sunny, and many of the townfolk were busily going about their errands. She nodded at a few gentlemen that walked by and proceeded to the sidewalk. Mary didn't have the standing in the town that Lucy had enjoyed, though they had married the same man. Lucy had hosted parties and luncheons and teas. She had servants and often had friends come to call. She played the piano and sang. People had been drawn to her. Mary was an afterthought. People were polite. There had been friends calling at first, mostly John's friends, and they would have dinner parties. But John had started to isolate himself more and more and the friends were tired of having their inquiries ignored. Mary felt that they blamed her for his change in mood. If only she had been more beautiful, more talented, more poised. Most ladies sent their servants to the market. For Mary, it was an opportunity to break free from the isolation of living with John. Even the slightest chance for a quiet "hello" or a tip of the hat lifted her spirits.

She headed south, down Main Street, breathing in the smells and taking in the sights. Carriages moved like trained cattle up and down the roadway, women bustled about, their skirts brushing against each other as they passed on the sidewalk. She could hear laughter, and the whistle of the train approaching, and happy conversations.

The bell on the door jingled, announcing her entrance into the market. She slowly walked up and down the few aisles of goods, pausing intermittently to take a longer look at things like laundry soap and baking flour. She purchased some soap, lantern oil, and a sack of rice. The proprietor was a friendly man and he smiled as he packed her belongings into her basket. He thanked her for her business and she smiled in return.

Outside the train riders were departing the train, spilling out onto the sidewalks and into the shops. A few folks were waiting to board, moving on to Charlotte for bigger and better shops or an evening at the theater. Mary longed for an evening at the theater, to watch a ballet or hear an opera. But John never mentioned such things and she didn't dare ask. Instead, she continued on down the road to the butcher shop to make her purchases there.

Finley returned promptly with the carriage, hefted her purchases up onto the carriage seat, then helped Mary board. He made pleasant conversation with her for a moment, inquiring as to her shopping and if she had met any friends. She politely answered in short sentences as she settled back into her seat. Finley returned to his perch upfront and urged the horses homeward.

John came out from his study as Mary entered the kitchen. He took her hand and gently kissed it, looking into her eyes with a mischievous smile.

"Ah, there is my beautiful wife. How was your shopping, darling?" he inquired, still holding her hand.

Mary was taken aback. She froze, not knowing how to react.

"Oh come now, Mary. Are you not still upset about this afternoon? I was just grumpy from a loss in my business dealings. You understand, don't you Mary dear?"

Mary managed an awkward smile and opened her mouth to speak. He held up a finger to quiet her.

"Come, I've got a surprise for you. Close your eyes and come with me into the parlor."

She followed as he requested, eyes closed, clutching his arm for support, her heart beating rapidly as various scenarios of this "surprise" flashed through her mind. He guided her to one of the wing-back chairs that faced the fireplace.

"Open your eyes, darling" he encouraged.

Mary opened her eyes and gasped in surprise. The wall above the fireplace had remained bare since John had taken down the portrait of Lucy to hang in his study. Where the bare wall had been now hung a beautiful portrait of Black-eyed Susans, Mary's favorite.

She looked up at her husband. "John, it's beautiful! But how....when?"

"I had it commissioned on my last trip to Charlotte. I know you love Black-eyed Susans, but they aren't in season now, and this way you can have flowers year-round." He smiled.

Mary thought her heart would explode. She rose and placed her head on his chest, wrapping her arms around his waist like a child. He held her tightly and whispered loving words in her ear.

He moved her back at arm's length and looked at her earnestly. "Then you're pleased? I'm so glad. Come, let's have a drink to celebrate our new happiness"

Mary sat back in her chair as John crossed to the pitcher on the kitchen table to pour sweet tea. He held a glass out to his wife, which she took with a demure smile.

John lifted his glass "To my wife" he smiled.

She smiled shyly and took a drink, letting her guard down, and enjoying the moment with John. They sat, in happy silence, sipping their drinks and watching the fire. Mary felt content for the first time in a long time. John refreshed their drinks, despite Mary's trying to wave him off. He told stories of his childhood and they laughed and smiled at each other. She felt such love for John at that moment. Then she felt nothing.

Mary awoke in her bed the next morning to the sounds of the servants already at work. She had never slept so soundly in all her life. She stretched and then rose from the bed. She walked to the table near the window that held the pitcher and water and poured a bit into the bowl. She splashed her face with the cool water and patted it dry with a towel. Feeling a bit more refreshed, she dressed and headed down to the main floor of the house.

Agnes, the kitchen maid, was busy readying the fire and preparing the bread. "Good Morning, Mrs. Ashton" she murmured politely.

"Good morning, Agnes. Sorry, I must have overslept, let me get my apron and help you."

"No, thank you, Mrs. Mr. Ashton requested that you have a day of rest. He said he'd be back from Charlotte for a late dinner."

Mary was taken aback. A day of rest? Then she remembered their light-hearted conversation the night before. The loving look in his eye. The warmth of the room. She hugged herself and smiled.

Up in her room, she grabbed her journal and sat at her desk facing the window. She opened the sash to let in a little of the fresh April air. With the sun shining and the sounds of the small farm around her, she began to write.

Love, love has returned to me! John is back, his demons are at rest and he is my lover once again. My heart is soaring like the crows from the fields. My prayers have been answered and our love grows. Blessings are forthcoming, I can feel it. Thank you, Dearest God, for bringing my lover back to me.

Mary sat back and breathed in the air, a smile on her lips. Then she grimaced. Her forehead began to sweat and she felt sick to her stomach. She ran to the basin on the table by her far window and vomited straight into it. The contents of her stomach mixed with the water and splashed onto the floor. She held onto the table, a dizzying feeling overtaking her. She called for the maid.

When John arrived home that evening, he found Mary in bed. The doctor had been called and had made his diagnosis.

"Mary, darling. What ails you sweetest? Agnes just told me that the doctor paid a visit." His brows were furrowed with concern.

"Dear Husband," Mary said softly "It's simply...it's the most wonderful news. Dr. Aney examined me and I am with child! I am with child" She wept with tears of joy.

John leaned in and kissed her forehead, "Oh my sweet, sweet girl. A baby. Oh Glory to God! I'm to be a father at last!"

They held each other closely, intermittently crying and laughing, until Mary felt fatigued. John changed into his dressing gown and climbed into bed with her, forgetting his dinner. He held her close as she fell asleep, smiling.

The next few months were a blur. Mary's belly grew and the midwife visited regularly. With John's parents having passed years ago, and Mary's mother tending to her older sister's troubles, Mary was mostly alone in her journey. It didn't bother her though. She spent her days getting the nursery ready and sewing tiny baby clothes. She went to town for yarn and knitted some baby blankets then used the leftover fabric from the clothes to sew a little quilt. John brought home a beautiful bassinet to keep by her bed. Mary was over the moon with happiness.

The midwife was called to the house at about 8 in the morning on January the 15th and the baby was born healthy and safe by lunchtime. John and Mary welcomed their daughter, Abigail with tears of joy, and John with cigars for his colleagues and servants.

Mary recovered well from birth and was particularly suited for motherhood. She doted on the child, as John doted on them both, and there was new happiness in the Ashton household. Little Abigail Rose was an adorable child with her mother's dark curls and her father's brown eyes.

Around the time that the baby was four months, John began working later and later in Charlotte. Mary was exhausted but happy and baby Abigail was flourishing. They would spend their days in the garden, snuggling and watching the clouds move or the crows swoop and dart through the sky. John suggested that Mary hire a governess or nanny, stating that Mary was far too consumed with the baby. Mary ignored him and continued to spend her days with her daughter.

It was around September that Mary began to fall ill. It started with what the doctor described as an acid stomach for which he gave Mary a chalky medicine to drink with meals. The stomach pain would come and go, and Mary would roll between being tired and being full of life. Through it all, she continued to be a good mother to Abigail. When she had her bad days, they would spend time quietly with books and small toys in the nursery. On her good days, they would venture out to the garden or she would put Abigail in the pram and walk her up and down the country road to the pond at the corner. There they would find dragonflies and ducks and Abigail would smile and coo at the strange and wondrous creatures.

John continued to work long hours in Charlotte, but that was counterbalanced by his loving nature upon return. He would dote on Mary and Abigail, bringing Mary sweet tea and biscuits while they talked about their days. Mary was so content, so happy with her little family. It had been months since she'd seen the dark cloud John's deep brown eyes, months since he had been seduced by the evils of alcohol. Those times seemed like an eternity ago.

Mary found herself becoming more and more of

an invalid. Doctors were called to the home on almost a weekly basis and she was pale and weak and nauseous nearly most of each week. The doctor noted on occasion that her pulse was weak and that she had a definite nervous affliction. Mary began to vomit, sometimes bringing blood. John was concerned, Lucy had died of consumption. Would he be losing his new bride to this devil of a disease as well? The doctor assured him that the symptoms were not consistent with consumption. Women, he stated, were naturally frail creatures. It was just the nature of life. He prescribed laudanum for her nerves and gave instructions to call on him if her condition worsened.

Mary insisted on sitting up in the parlor most days, even when she was taken ill, so that she could greet John when he arrived home and they would enjoy their sweet tea and stories. She had magazines brought from the market, Godey Lady's Book, and Leslie's Illustrated so that she had something to thumb through and occupy her mind.

That weekend, Mary spent much of her day in her room in bed. Nausea and vomiting had gotten worse and she was nearly doubled over in pain. She prayed nightly to the Virgin Mary to help ease her suffering, but it continued on nonetheless. She was laying in bed, looking out the window at the birds and the changing leaves when a particularly sharp pain in her abdomen caught her off guard. She tried to call for the maid, but her voice was weak. She tried to reach for the basin near her bed and knocked it to the floor. She eased her feet over the side of the bed and sunk to the floor near the basin and began to get sick. Nausea rolled over her like waves and she retched and vomited and could barely catch her breath. Bright red trails were left on the sleeves of her sleeping gown where she wiped her mouth between heaves. Desperate, she began to bang on the floor. She could hear footsteps on the stairs and John burst into the room, finding his wife on the floor amid a pool of blood and other fluids. She was pale and drawn. Mary looked to her husband for reassurance but found only terror in his eyes. He yelled for the maid and reached a hand toward Mary's shoulder. The maid came in carrying towels and another basin. She knelt on the floor with her mistress and rubbed her back as Mary swayed back and forth. Just then Abigail began to cry in the nursery.

"Mr. Ashton, would you like me to tend to Abigail?" Agnes asked.

"Yes, please do" he answered.

John turned his attention to Mary as Agnes slipped out the door. She reached the nursery and carefully pushed the door open. Reaching into Abigail's crib, she picked her up and held her close.

"Hush, hush sweet girl. You'll be fine. It's almost over...it's almost over".

A priest was called the next morning, to sit with Mary as she lay semi-conscious in bed. Dr. Aney had already come and gone, administering morphine for the pain and shaking his head at the state of his patient.

"I don't know, I just don't know, Mr. Ashton," the doctor remarked, "I think she may have a ruptured ulcer. Sometimes, these things heal themselves. All we can do is wait. Pray, and wait."

John nodded solemnly. Agnes was tending to Abigail, so he went to his study to think. His wife may be dying. He mulled that over in his head. His wife may be dying. He poured himself a drink, walked to the window, and looked out over his land. A single crow flew by and settled in the tree nearest the flower garden. It seemed to be watching him, an accusatory look to its eye. John stared back at the bird, daring it to comment.

Around four o'clock, John went to the kitchen. Agnes was busy readying for teatime.

"I was just about to take some to the Mrs", she said aloud.

"I'll take care of that. I should check in on her anyhow" John remarked.

Agnes looked at him, curtsied, and left the room.

John carried the tray that held the tea and biscuits---just in case Mary felt like eating a little---up to the bedroom. He knocked softly on the door and could hear Mary stirring. She was awkwardly trying to sit up as he entered and her face lit up when she saw him.

"John…" she said weakly and tried to smile.

He placed the tea tray on the table next to her and offered her a warm cup. She brought it shakily to her lips and sipped. They sat in silence for a few minutes while she quenched her thirst. How she wanted him to hold her, comfort her. But he stood straight at the edge of her bed, watching her like a science experiment.

"How are you feeling, my love?" he inquired.

Mary took a deep, shaky breath and coughed. A little bit of blood spilled from her lips and she hastily dried it up with her handkerchief.

"I'll be fine" she whispered and smiled at him. He smiled back, but his eyes were vacant.

"Abigail?" she winced as she spoke.

"She's doing well. She spent most of the after-noon in the garden with Agnes. Don't worry about her, just concentrate on getting well, dear." he answered.

Mary held her cup out to him and he placed it on the tea tray. She shifted her weight and slid back down on the pillow, pulling the covers up around her chin.

"Sleep now" whispered John.

Mary closed her eyes as John turned and walked out of the room.

The next morning brought with its gray skies and drizzle. A gentle wind swayed the trees, making it look as though they were weeping women, rocking in their grief. Mary hadn't woken that morning. She had passed some time in the early morning. The front of her nightgown and her bed linens were spattered with the blood she had coughed up in the night. Her skin was pale and drawn and cold to the touch. Agnes had discovered the horrible scene and shrieked, alerting John. He had rushed upstairs, and upon discovering his wife's demise, closed her eyes and pulled the bedsheet up to cover her face. He did not shed a tear or tenderly caress her hand. He ordered Agnes to alert Thomas as to what had occurred, and send him into town to fetch Dr. Aney. Agnes, with a long glance at Jon, left the room. She removed the tea tray from the night before and headed to the kitchen. She found Thomas drinking coffee out back and relayed the news. Then she went back inside and quietly hummed a lullaby as she rinsed the cup and teapot and set them to the side of the sink. Then she went to the pantry and reached back behind the canned goods. She pulled a canister of rodent poison out from behind the cans and took it out to the dustbin around the back of the house. She buried it under the trash on top, then, wiping her hands on her pants, she went back inside to the study to tend to her love.

Made in the USA
Columbia, SC
13 February 2021